Missing

Penelope Jonas

Contents

Chapter One

Luke's POV.

"Luke, go get changed and get your camera ready!" Beau shouted from the kitchen, his words were muffled by his mouthful of toast. I rolled my eyes but nodded, dragging myself up to mine and Jai's shared bedroom.

I scavenged through the pile of clothes that had been messily dumped on the computer chair. Me and Jai usually just dumped our clothes onto the chair instead of actually putting them into the washing basket, but hey, if it smelt clean, it was clean. I pulled out a plain white shirt along with a pair of black jeans. I turned around, startled slightly as I saw Jai sat on his bed. He was staring blankly at me, no expression on his face whatsoever.

"You alright?" I questioned, raising an eyebrow at him. He simply nodded. I had no idea what was up with him, he was fine a few hours ago. I shrugged it off though, I didn't want to pester him about it. Yet.

After I had gotten changed, I grabbed my backpack from the closet before retrieving my camera, phone and earphones and stuffing them in there. Grabbing a black beanie and placing it neatly onto my hair. "Coming?" I asked as I turned to face Jai. He got up from his bed and followed closely behind me as we joined the boys.

The boys sat ready and waiting in the living room, all of them snacking on an apple each. "Are you ready now?" Beau questioned, I nodded before swinging my backpack over my shoulders.

"This is so exciting" Daniel squealed like a four year old school girl, Beau chuckled at him.

"Let's go!" James fist pumped the air as we all left the house and piled into Beau's car. Beau driving whilst Daniel taxed the passenger seat and me, Jai and James all squashed in the back.

"Who's ready to meet some ghosts!" Beau yelled before starting the engine. We all cheered, we all of us except for Jai. Jai may be a huge believer in ghosts but he didn't seem too keen on our late night outing. But Beau had just about managed to convince him to come with us.

The orange street lights lit up the road as the car started moving. It was 11pm, most people wouldn't be out and about at this time so the roads were quiet.

Beau turned up the radio as we drove to our destination, all of us sang along to the hit tunes, again, all of us except Jai.

He rested his head his hand as he gazed out of the window, an unreadable expression on his face. I nudged his side slightly, grabbing his attention. "Are you okay?" I whispered quiet enough for only the two of us to hear. He nodded slightly before shooting me a small side smile.

I wasn't convinced but I didn't want to push him to tell me so I shrugged it off.

"I bet a hundred dollars that Beau will piss himself." Daniel snickered as he turned in his seat to face the three of us. James nodded with a smirk as he agreed with him. "Hey! Stop picking on me!" Beau chuckled as he glanced at us through the rearview mirror. He returned his gaze back to the road as the car slowly began to fall into a peaceful silence.-

"Beau are we there yet." Daniel whined, we had been driving for almost an hour now. The car was silent, James was listening to his music through his earphones, Jai had fallen asleep and Daniel and Beau were talking about god knows what. For the entire ride here and the two hours before we had left, Jai hadn't spoken a word.

"We will be arriving in three...two...one" Beau announced before pulling up in an empty parking lot.

Daniel sighed in relief before he, Beau and James hopped out of the car. I nudged Jai again slightly,waking him up. "Come on, we're here" I chuckled at his sleepy state. He rubbed his eyes slightly before letting out a big yawn. The both of us jumped out of the car, joining the other boys.

The tall building stood in darkness in front of us. The brickwork was slowly wasting away, almost every window had been smashed up, a piece of wood covering most of them, there was trash littered around every inch of the building and a huge sign that read 'West Gate Asylum" dangled at an angle. It was safe to say the place had been abandoned for a good few years.

"Beau you can go in first, it was your idea to come here." James suggested, causing all of us to snicker at Beau's uneasy expression.

"Nah I'm good, we'll go in together" He laughed nervously.

I pulled out my camera from my backpack and began recording all of us boys. "Hey guys, we're the Janoskians!" We all announced. "And today, we're exploring an abandoned insane asylum! We'll be recording our findings!" Beau added.

We began walking towards the entrance of the building, trash and twigs crunching underneath our feet with each step we took.

The entrance doors had been boarded up but luckily there was a slight gap big enough for us to squeeze through. Daniel peaked through the gap, being met with nothing but darkness. "I vote Beau to go in first" Daniel said as he pushed Beau forwards. "Why me!" Beau exclaimed, pushing Daniel back playfully. "It was your idea to come here!".

"You're a bunch of wimps! I'll go first, last one in is a Beau!" James mumbled before squeezing through the gap. "Hey!" Beau yelled with a chuckle. We all followed one by one through the small gap. Beau flicked on a torch, illuminating the buildings interior. It looked exactly how I expected it to look. The once white walls were chipping away, revealing the under layer of brickwork, medical tools and stretchers were dumped almost everywhere, patient records were ripped up and scattered across the floors and not to mention the amount of graffiti covering the floors and walls.

"Damn look at this place" I muttered, the condition of it was expected but still shocking. The Asylum had been built many years ago, so there's no doubt that the patients who lived here were treated badly. "I know, it's so old" Daniel nodded.

Jai shivered slightly as he gazed at the site, he had yet to say a single word but I still chose not to question it. I would probably try and pry whatever was bothering him out of him when we got home.

"Let's start exploring." James sighed, we descended further into the building, stepping over pieces of equipment that had been left of the floor. I panned my camera to different parts of the building, trying to capture all of the scenery.

"So this is the first floor of the building and there's three floors, are we going to explore it all tonight?" Beau questioned. "Why not." I shrugged, earning nods of approval from James and Daniel.

"So when do we start asking the ghosts questions and stuff?" Daniel carelessly asked, scratching the back of his neck. In response, Beau slapped Daniels arm harshly. "Shut up! They'll hear you" He hissed through his teeth. Beau turned away from us, shining the light at different objects. Me, James and Daniel snickered at Beau whilst Jai just stared blankly at him.

We wondered further into the building, Jai was close by my side, his arm brushing against mine every now and then.

The graffiti soon became unsettling the further into the building we got, satanic symbols had been drawn along the walls along with various words in different languages.

"What's in there?" James questioned. He carefully opened a wooden door which was hanging off of its hinges. We all stumbled into the room, glancing around as Beau shon his torch around. In the middle of the room was a thin bed with rusty machinery placed besides it, along with a metal table placed on the opposite side. The Windows had been smashed and the graffiti had followed us into the room as well.

We scuffled around the room as we picked up different pieces of equipment.

"What's this?" Jai questioned in a quiet voice, he picked up two small metal poles from the table, it still had wiring connecting to it. "Jai but that down!" James gasped, snatching the poles from Jai's hand before dumping them on the table. "What is it?" Beau repeated Jai's unanswered questioned. "I think this is the room where they electrocuted patients and those were the probes they used." James spoke, cautiously poking at the machinery.

"What are you getting freaked out about? This stuff hasn't been used in ages, I doubt it still works." Daniel chuckled as he picked up the two probes, playfully pointing them at Jai as they both chuckled slightly. James snatched the tools from Daniels hands before dumping them onto the table once again.

"Come on you fools, let's see what else is here." Beau laughed.

Beau led us out of the room as we explored various different rooms, a lot of them were different private rooms where sick patients would stay. We walked down the hallway, being careful of the trash that was scattered everywhere. The only thing lightening this place us was the flashlight Beau had been using, but even that didn't light enough of it up. Every now and then one of us would accidentally trip up on different objects that were lying around.

The further into the building we got, the more unsettled I felt. I don't know if it was because we had ventured further away from the nearest exited so we couldn't make a quick escape, or if it was because this place truly was haunted.

I filmed the floor, capturing all of the rubble that had been carelessly left behind, panning up to the wall, I filmed all of the graffiti that had been drawn. It was easy to tell just by the condition of the building that it held thousands of horrifying stories.

"Hey guys, look at me." Daniel giggled childishly. Turning around, we all faced Daniel who wore a giant grin on his face along with an old tatty nurses hat on top of his head, he posed in a girly fashion. We all burst out into laughter at the sight of him.

"Oh doctor save me!" Beau dramatically yelled as he threw himself into Daniels arms. I rolled my eyes with a smile as the two finished up their little 'scene.'

"Okay now that was fun-" James was cut off by a loud bang echoing through the halls. I felt Jai jump behind me as he tightly gripped onto my arm. The colour had basically drained from all of our faces as the echo began to fade. I could physically feel Jai shaking slightly as we all stood dead silent.

"What the hell was that?" Daniel whispered nervously. We all glanced between each other, mentally searching for some kind of explanation. "I think we made it angry Beau." Daniel whispered, his eyes were filled with fear.

"Haha! I got you guys so good!" Jai burst out into fits of laughter. The four of us stared at him with nervous smiles as we began to process that the loud bang we had heard was created by Jai and not some evil entity. That's always good to know.

Jai being quiet this entire time was part of his plan, so he could scare the living daylight out of us later on.

We eventually began laughing as Beau playfully pushed Jai backwards by his shoulders. Pulling him into a gentle headlock, I ruffled his hair as he laughed hysterically. "You jerk.".

"You got us good." James chuckled as he patted Jai on the back.

-

We had finally ventured to the second floor of the building, it looked almost identical to the first floor except this was where the mentally ill patients were held. There were many small rooms with tatty bed frames. I had read a report on how many of these patients had been mistreated on the second floor. They were kept in their small room with just an uncomfortable bed for hours and hours, they were only fed small meals twice a day. Many of them had committed suicide by slamming their heads off of the brick walls.

"This floor looks even creepier." Jai whispered, even though he had thought it was funny to scare us, he was still scared himself as he clung to my side nervously.

"Is that blood?!" Daniel shrieked, pointing towards a wall in one of the small rooms. A trail of dried red liquid had stained the wall. "Shut up skip!" Beau once again hissed. He felt that we were 'disrespecting' the spirits.

"Is anyone here with us?" James questioned as we came to a halt, hoping to catch at least something before we left. The halls were silent, only a white noise was heard. "Move something if you're here." I yelled slightly. We listened carefully for any kind of noise.

A few minutes later a small pebble was thrown down the dark hallway, bouncing towards us before it landed in front of Jai's feet.

"Holy crap." James whispered, we stared at the small pebble for a few seconds. I glanced down the hallway, pointing my camera in the same direction in hopes to capture anything. "Here, hold my camera." I gestured to Beau as I handed him my camera. I pulled my phone from my backpack pocket, opening up the camera and activating the flash. I snapped a few pictures of the pitch black hallway before swiping through some of them.

"Did you get anything?" Daniel questioned, I shook my head in response. I had taken about 5 pictures and so far none of them showed any signs of something paranormal.

Jai leaned over as he observed the photos. I swiped to the last photo gasping slightly. I had captured Jai in the photo but surrounding him was a slight mist, it looked as if the most had wrapped itself around Jai's body. Jai mimicked my response as he gasped at the photo.

"What? What did you get?" James asked, snatching my phone from my hand as he, Beau and Daniel examined the photo with wide eyes. "Dude, that's mad!".

"Make a loud noise if you're here with us!" Beau demanded.

Another loud bang bounced off of the walls, we all laughed slightly knowing it was just Jai messing around with us again.

"Ha ha, very funny Jai." I chuckled softly, though when I received no response I quickly turned around coming face to face with nothing but darkness. I quickly scanned my surroundings, but Jai was no where to be seen.

"Jai?!".

Chapter Two

Luke's POV.

"Jai! Where are you?!" I yelled in frustration, my voice bounced off of almost every wall in this building so there was no way he couldn't hear me. The place was dead silent, even our footsteps could be heard from the opposite end of the building.

I kicked the rubble out of my way as I frantically searched for Jai, I had no care whether I was 'disturbing' whatever the hell was here, I just needed to find Jai.

I tugged at my hair harshly as the only things that came into sight was darkness. I looked behind every closed doors in hopes to see him, I looked behind all of the larger machinery, I had practically searched the entire second floor. Along with the other boys help of course.

"Luke he's probably just playing a prank on us, just calm down bro." Beau chuckled. But for some reason, his words lit a flame inside me. Jai was nowhere to be seen and he thinks it's funny?. I scowled slightly before picking up the nearest object and lunging it at Beau. He jumped back in shock at my sudden burst of anger, even I was shocked but right now I couldn't care less.

"Woah woah Luke, calm down we'll find him." James attempted to comfort me, he pulled me backwards, creating a distance between me and Beau as he rubbed my back softly, Daniel just simply stood back.

"Come on, Beau and Daniel will search the first floor and me and you will search the third floor." James smiled, he gestured me away from the two boys before we made our way to the third floor.

The staircase that led there looked as if it could collapse at anytime, it had been made out of wood and due to the rain that poured into the building after several years, the wood had weakened. It didn't look safe but at this point I was willing to do anything.

"Luke I don't think that's sa-" James began but before he had the chance to finish his sentence I had already sprinted to the top of the staircase. With each step I took the staircase creaked, bits of dust and rubble fell to the ground.

James stood at the bottom of the staircase gazing up at me, I could tell by his facial expression that he was debating whether or not he should risk running up the stairs as well.

"Just run as fast as you can." I mumbled impatiently.

James closed his eyes as he sucked in a deep breath before copying my actions and sprinting up. Only this time, my previous weight had weakened the staircase even more, which meant as James reached the top, the stair case completely demolished into a huge pile.

We both looked down with wide eyes, either one of us could've been halfway up that staircase as it collapsed, but lucky for us we weren't. But like I said, I was willing to take risks for Jai.

"Great! Now how are we supposed to get back down!" James yelled out in frustration, he ran his hands through his hair as he tugged at the ends. "We'll find a way." I sighed softly, tugging James by the back of his shirt.

There had to be some other staircase or exit at least that'll help, I'm sure this place would have a emergency exit in case of a fire or something. But that wasn't my main priority at the moment.

The third floor looked exactly the same as the second, I'm guessing this is where the severely mentally ill patients were held. Again, there were old medical tools scattered across the floor along with more patient files. The wall paper had been completely stripped, the floor was damp along with a few rain puddles that had been created in different corners. Huge metal pipes were dangling from what was left of the ceiling.

The hallway was dead silent, not a single noise, you could probably hear a pin drop in here.

"Do you think he's up here?" I questioned James nervously, if he wasn't on this floor or the second floor and if Beau and Daniel can't find him on the first floor then I'm pretty sure I'd have a nervous break down.

"I have no idea." James sighed, I could hear the sadness in his voice.

I swallowed the huge lump that formed in my throat, the thought of leaving this place without Jai made me feel sick to my stomach. I wouldn't be able to sleep in my bed knowing that Jai was out in the cold night on his own, probably scared.

We searched every room we passed in hopes of finding him, but nothing. All we were met with was a bunch of trash. Panic began setting in as I realised we had almost searched the entire third floor and there was no trace of Jai.

Suddenly a door slammed shut, I'm guessing that the force of the slam had knocked the door off of its hinges judging by the loud thud that followed.

Both James and I jumped out of our skin at the bang, I sucked in a deep breath as I chuckled softly. That had to be Jai slamming the door, this was probably just part of his 'prank'. The soft giggling that filled the air almost confirmed my theory.

"I think he's in there!" James chuckled as we followed the sounds of the soft giggles. The giggling lead us to the same room where the door had slammed shut as it was lying flat on the floor. As we approached the room, the giggling came to a halt.

"Jai come on, stop playing!" I grinned as I poked my head into the room expecting to see Jai, though I was filled with nothing but disappointment. The room was bare, no one or nothing in sight.

-

We had searched the entire asylum top to bottom, the four of us retraced each other's steps just to make sure we hadn't missed anything but not a single sign of Jai.

"Come on let's just go home." Beau sighed as he glanced around, he picked his back back up off of the floor before swinging it across his shoulders. I felt so much anger towards Beau, how can he just want to leave this place without knowing where Jai is? What if he's lost in here somewhere? He'll be so scared if we leave him.

"We can't leave until we find Jai!" I spat harshly.

"He's probably just messing around with us, I bet you this is all some kind of prank, he probably made his way home!" Beau laughed before rolling his eyes.

"But what if he's not at home Beau!" I cried in frustration, I couldn't bare the thought of leaving Jai out in the cold night on his own.

"Well he's not here Luke! We've searched the entire place and not one of us has found him!" Beau groaned, he didn't even seem concerned for Jai or his safety and that's what angered me most. Because in Beau's mind this was all a big joke.

"Are you even worried about him? Our brother has just disappeared and you don't even care!".

"I'm not worried because this is all one big joke, now come on let's go home!".

-

It took about two hours to actually convince me to leave and go home and by convince I mean dragged home. Beau kept reassuring me that this was all a big prank, even though I didn't agree with him, I just nodded along. I was convinced that Jai was still in that building and we had left him there. I'd never be able to forgive myself. I can't even imagine how scared he'd be.

We pulled up into the driveway seeing that the living room lights were still lit even though it was probably 3am. We had dropped James and Daniel off on our way home and now it was just me, Beau and an awkward silence. Neither of us had spoken a word to each other, I was still angry at him for making us leave without finding Jai.

We hopped out of the car before Beau locked it, tiredly stumbling into the house, Beau and I were pulled into a tight hug.

"I was so worried! Where the hell were you!" Our mum cried as she pulled us close.

We hadn't told her where we were going because she wouldn't allow us if she knew we were visiting an alleged haunted asylum, we hadn't even planned to stay at the asylum that long but we spent an extra few hours looking for Jai.

We pulled away from the hug as she planted a kiss on both of our cheeks. I felt terrible for worrying her so much.

"Where's Jai?" She questioned, she glanced behind both of us as she scanned the driveway for him. And that was when my heart dropped out of my chest and into my stomach. Jai wasn't home, he wasn't safe and warm at home. He was still missing.

Chapter Three

Luke's POV

Beau, mum and I sat gathered around the small wooden table. An eerie silence filled the air. I knew that mum was disappointed in us but right now her main concern was Jai. She stared at the table with dull eyes, she had been crying for the past hour or so and to say I felt guilty was an understatement.

She sucked in a deep breath before her gaze met mine and Beau's. Her eyes were read and puffy and her cheeks were stained with tears.

"Did you look for him?" She question, her voice was extremely shaky. She crossed her hands in front of her on the table as she awaited our answer.

"We looked everywhere, we even split up into groups." Beau replied, the sadness and guilt was practically dripping from his words.

Beau has considered bending the truth about what had happened, I knew he was scared to get into trouble since he's the oldest. But bending the truth wouldn't help us find Jai, mum needed to know every single bit of detail, even if that resulted in us being grounded for the rest of our lives.

Mum rubbed her hands up and down her face, she was terrified, as were me and Beau. The drive to the asylum took an hour, which meant that Jai was lost and alone in an unfamiliar place. And to add onto that, the weather wasn't on our side either.

"Why did you go? Beau you're supposed to set an example for them!" Mum suddenly yelled, her hands slammed down onto the table as a look of anger washed over her features.

Beau looked down at his hands as he avoided her gaze. Even though Beau was a daring person, he wasn't used to getting into trouble, especially by mum. The last time mum was this angry was when we were little.

"I'm sorry." Mum whispered, both Beau and I remained silent, not knowing what to say.

"Can't we just call the police?" I spoke up in a small voice, I just needed my brother back. I refused to allow myself to sleep in my bed tonight knowing that Jai was out in the cold.

"He has to be missing for twenty four hours before the police can do anything." She shook her head as she sniffled.

Anger burned in the pit of my stomach. I had read somewhere that the first twenty four hours of a disappearance was the most crucial, the missing person is most likely to be killed in the first twenty four hours. Though we didn't even know if Jai had been taken, the fact that the police weren't concerned about my brothers safety angered me greatly.

"And what if he's dead by then!' I suddenly yelled, causing Beau and mum to jump. I didn't mean to frighten them, but in these situations, my frustration and anger always got the best of me.

I pushed the chair I was sitting in backwards harshly, storming out of the living room, up the stairs and into Jai and i's bedroom.

I slammed the door shut behind me before throwing myself into Jai's bed. And that's when I let the tears fall, I couldn't keep them in any longer, the worry, panic and anger had taken over me. I ran my hands through my hair, tugging harshly at the ends before I threw the nearest object at the wall in front of me.

I took deep breaths, try to calm myself down as I watched the object I had thrown bounce off of the wall and land in front of me. That said object was Jai's sketch book.

My gaze was fixed on the black hard back sketch book, I knew that a lot of things he had drawn in here were personal. I picked up the book, mentally debating whether I should peak through it or not. I don't think Jai would mind, we shared everything with each other, but it still felt as if I were invading his privacy.

My curiosity got the best of me as I began skimming through the pages, every sketch had been drawn to perfection with a simple pencil, the creativity in his drawings was amazing. I knew he liked to doodle around, but I honestly had no idea he was this talented.

I came across a page at the back of the sketch book, he had drawn a rose with a ribbon wrapped around the stem. Written on the ribbon in cursive writing was our names. Beau, Luke and Jai. I remembered how proud he was of this drawing, he kept asking me to take a look but I always blew him off. The guilt instantly washed over me as my brain flashed back to that moment.

-"Luke! Look at what I drew!" Jai ran into our bedroom holding his sketch pad tightly in his hands. I groaned as I plugged my earphones in and turned onto my side, trying to concentrate on the video that was playing on my phone.

"Come on Luke! It takes two seconds, just take a look." He chuckled softly. I could feel the bunk shake slightly as he climbed up the ladder.

He sat on top of me as he obnoxiously yanked my earphones out. How was I supposed to edit this damn video when Jai kept pestering me about his drawings. I sighed softly before pushing him off of me carefully. "Stop Jai! I need to edit this new video." I scolded, I could see the excitement fade from his face as he slowly backed off.

"I'm sorry, I just wanted you to see my drawing." He mumbled sadly as began crawling back down the ladder before exiting the room.

I sighed softly, plugging my ear phones back in before turning back onto my side as I continued to edit the video.

-

The guilt practically ate me alive. I should've payed attention to him, I ruined his excitement. Remembering the look on his face as he left the room in disappointment will continue to haunt me.

I stared down at the picture as I gently traced my hand over it, a small tear drop landed on the bottom of the page. It's moments like this when you realise how much you take people for granted. I definitely took Jai for granted and only now I'm realising it, I just needed him to be okay.

I was pulled out of my thought by my phone vibrating in my pocket, I sniffled slightly as I placed the sketch pad to the side before slipping my phone out of my pocket.

My eyes scanned the message over and over again, my heart dropping into my stomach as I processed the message.

'I'm gone.'

The message had been sent from Jai's phone, I shakily stood up from the bed as I trembled over to the desk, seeing Jai's phone placed on the computer chair. The message had been sent from Jai's phone, but Jai's phone was on the chair right in front of me.

Chapter Four

L uke's POV

I had been staring at the phone for what seemed like hours now, my brain just couldn't process what was happening. That text should be impossible to send, a text from Jai's number to Jai's phone. This stuff doesn't happen to people like us, it only happens in movies! I was still having trouble processing if all this was real or not. I knew Jai liked to pull pranks but I also knew he wouldn't take it this far.

I needed to show Beau the text. I shakily stood up from Jai's bunk with his phone firm in my grip before I quietly darted out of the bedroom and into the living room.

I scanned the living room, everything was turned off and in darkness. I huffed as I darted down the hallway and to Beau's room. I didn't even consider knocking on his door as I unintentionally slammed it open.

"You scared me." Beau jumped slightly as he breathed out, placing his hand on top of his chest. He was sat in his bed under his blankets with his laptop, the screen lit up his face as he stared up at me.

"Look at this." I demanded as I tip toed over the pieces of clothing and shoes scattered across his floor.

"Is that Jai's phone?" Beau questioned as he placed his laptop to the side. I nodded in response as I handed him the phone.

"Read the last text message." I spoke, sitting down on the end of his bed. I watched as Beau's eyes scanned across his face as I awaited his reaction. A look of confusion.

"The last text was sent by you Luke?" He raised his eyebrow as he glanced up at me. Furrowing my eyebrows I snatched the phone from his hands as I inspected the messages. The last text was indeed sent from me, but where the heck did the mystery text go?! I scanned through drafts and deleted messages but the text had been completely erased.

How is that even possible? I didn't even delete the message and now it's gone!

"N-no there was a message from Jai's number sent to his phone! It said 'I'm gone'" I stuttered as I frantically searched the phone. Beau's features held a saddened look as he breathed out a sigh.

"It's been a tough day Luke, you're tired." He smiled sadly as he stood up from his bed, gently placing his hands on my shoulders.

"Beau I swear!" My voice cracked slightly as my eyes began to fill with tears. I felt frustrated and upset, I needed Jai to be okay and I needed Beau to see that message.

"If it makes you feel any better, I gave the police Jai's details and I'm making posters with his face on them, we can hang them up around town tomorrow." Beau sighed softly as he gently patted my back.

I glanced at his computer screen to see a missing person poster with Jai's face and details written on it. Just the sight of the posted made me choke on a sob, it was slowly becoming more and more real to me.

Beau pulled me into a tight comforting hug as I spilt out my emotions I had been holding in. I sobbed onto his shoulder as he reassuring rubbed my back.

"I'm not crazy, I saw the message." I whimpered into his shoulder, my voice came out muffled. Beau pulled me back, his arms still resting on my arms as he stared at me.

"The only message on Jai's phone is from you bud."

Chapter Five

Luke's POV

I had tossed and turned all night, I hadn't got any sleep whatsoever. I couldn't sleep, I wouldn't let myself sleep. How could I sleep when Jai was lost in the dark cold night in an unfamiliar place. I sat up in Jai's bed for most of night just crying, I felt so helpless and useless. I wanted to help find him but I didn't even know where to begin. Melbourne is a big place, he could be anywhere. I don't even know if he ran away, got lost or if someone had taken him.

It was currently 6am, both Beau and I woke up extremely early to print off the posters he had made. We were going to drive back to the asylum and put up the posters around that location since that's where he was last.

Mum had also gotten up early but she took the day off of work so she could head to the police station to give more information about Jai. If he wasn't found by tonight then the police would send out a search party.

I gathered all of the posters that we had printed before stuffing them into my back pack. They basically had a recent picture of Jai with his appearance, information and our contact details listed underneath.

I sighed sadly as watched the printer spit out the last poster, seeing Jai's face on a missing persons poster just made my stomach churn. He should be home with us, playing video games and making YouTube videos. It scared me deeply that I have no idea what happened to him or whether I would see him again. I've spent my entire life with him by my side and I couldn't bare the thought of going through life without him.

I stuffed the last poster into my back pack before I swung it over my shoulders. As well as putting up the posters we were going to go back to the asylum and have another look since it was day light outside.

"Come on bud." Beau appeared from the kitchen as he patted my back, guiding me out of the house and into his car. I jumped into the front seat, buckling up whilst Beau jumped into the drivers seat.

We took off onto the main road in silence, the radios volume was on low as different songs mumbled through the speakers. It wasn't awkward silence, more like a sad one. Neither of us knew what to say to comfort each other, the only thing we could do was stare out onto the road ahead of us.

I sunk down into the seat, I had pulled my backpack off of my shoulders and held it tightly on my lap. I had a bit of hope that someone would recognise Jai's face from the posters and contact us, but I knew that anything could've happened within those few hours he's been missing. The asylum was located in a rough part of the city.

My mind wandered back to the text message that came through on Jai's phone last night. It was unexplained, and I'm pretty sure that Beau thought that I was hallucinating.

"What happens if us or the police can't find him?" I mumbled slightly, my gaze fixed on the car driving in front of us.

"Don't think like that Luke, you need to keep a positive mind." Beau scolded, he tightened his grip around the steering wheel slightly. I knew that I had to be strong, strong for Beau and mum and strong for Jai. But it was hard when I had no idea where he was or if he was even still alive for that matter.

Even if he hadn't been killed, he had no money with him, which meant if he was lost then he'd have no way of getting food or water.

Tears pricked at my eyes as different scenarios bombarded my brain, my heart beat physically sped up in sadness and fear.

"I miss him Beau, he's only been gone for a day and I miss him more than anything." I choked on a sob as I tried my best to get my words out. The tears spilled from my eyes and onto my cheeks. Sniffling slightly, I used the end of my sleeve to dry my eyes.

"We'll do everything we can to find him and the police will." Beau sighed, he didn't see, too confident with his words but how can he be. I just nodded in response as the remainder of the car ride fell into silence.

-

We finally pulled up into the parking lot of the asylum, the pebbles crunching underneath the tires. Unbuckling our belts as fast as we could, we both jumped out of the car in a hurry. I pulled the posters from out of my backpack before swinging the straps over my shoulders.

"We'll hang some of these posters up around the town and then we'll have another look in the asylum." Beau ordered.

We wandered away from the car and out onto the main road. We were in small town by the name of 'West Gate'. I bit my lip to prevent my tears as I pinned the first poster to the nearest lamp post. It still seemed surreal.

Whilst pinning the posters around the town, we asked the few occasional people if they had seen Jai anywhere, only to be given the same apologetic smile and shake of the head. We pinned some of the posters to shop windows, trees and we had placed a few of them on car windshields underneath the wipers.

My legs were beginning to ache from the amount of walking we were doing, but I couldn't careless. I would walk on a path of broken glass if it meant finding Jai.

I saw an elderly lady sat on a wooden rocking chair outside a small bakery, she looked as if she owned the shop judging by the long bib that was tied around her waist. I guessed she was taking a break due to the store being closed, and due to the fact that she was just knitting outside the store.

I slowly began to jog over to her, careful not the startle her. My shadow blocked the sunlight from beaming down on her face which drew her attention to me. She looked welcoming, her grey hair was held up with curlers which had been protected by a hair net, she wore silk floral clothing along with a thin pair of glasses that sat on the end of her nose.

"Excuse me ma'am, have you seen my brother?" I questioned politely before handing her the poster. She smiled warmly at me before her grey eyes scanned Jai's picture.

"Ah yes, this young man visited my store last night." Her face beamed with happiness as she gazed at the photo. My heart stopped in my chest. Jai was okay, well I hoped that he was still okay but this was process, we were getting closer to finding him.

"H-he was?" My voice shook as I spoke, I felt happiness for the first time in hours and a sort of relief.

"Yes, he seemed very afraid though, he kept telling me that 'they were after him'" She explained, her features washed with confusion as she mentally wondered what Jai had meant. What did he mean? Who were they? And why were they coming for him? That little bit of relief soon turned to worry, Jai was afraid and alone. Panic soon began setting in.

"Did he say who 'they' were?." I questioned, desperately hoping for at least some kind of information that could help us find Jai.

The little old lady shook her head with that same damn apologetic smile. She handed me back the poster before she set her knitting needles and ball of wool aside.

"He ran off into that building over there."

I looked in the direction she was pointing to see the West Gate Asylum standing behind some bare trees.

Chapter Six

L uke's POV

As soon as I saw the building that the little old lady had pointed at, I took off running. I felt rude for just suddenly abandoning the lady mid sentence but I hoped she understood. I roughly grabbed Beau by the hood of his jumper, pulling him with me as my legs carried me as fast as I could.

I didn't even have the time or breath to explain, my lungs were quickly running out of oxygen the quicker I ran but I ignored the burning sensation as I pushed myself to run faster.

He had to be in the asylum, that's were he was when he went missing and that's were the old lady said she seen him run. I mentally promised myself that I wouldn't be leaving without him this time. I will tear down every wall if it meant finding him.

I was thankful that Beau didn't even question why I had suddenly grabbed him and ran, he just went along with me and kept up with my pace.

The building came closer and closer the faster my legs worked, my chest began to tighten. I was trying my best to get as much air into my lungs as I possibly could as the burning sensation began soar throughout my chest violently. I felt my legs wobbling beneath me as I tried to maintain my speed.

I pounced over the metal fence that surrounding the building, Beau copying my actions as the fence shook slightly under our weight. I threw myself roughly over to the other side, landing onto my back with a harsh thump, Beau landed swiftly onto his feet.

Using the little amount of energy my body contained, I tried to push myself up off of the ground, little pebbles digging into my hands as I did so. But I was pushed back to the ground gently by Beau.

"Luke just breath for a few seconds, you're gonna collapse." He ordered as he knelt down in front of me. My breathing quickened as my heart rate tried its best to slow itself down. My knees ached, my chest burned and my head felt light.

He unzipped my back pack before pulling out a bottle of water, he unscrewed the cap before handing me the bottle. The cool water felt amazing, I poured some of it over my face, cooling myself down as I regained my breath.

"Come on." I whispered as I sucked in deep breaths, I carefully pulled myself up from the ground with the help of Beau. He held onto my arm as my knees shook with each step I took. I knew that I had overworked myself by running at a fast speed without stopping or slowing, but I needed to get into the asylum as soon as possible.

The building looked same, other than a few cracks into bricks that went unnoticed two days ago due to the night.

The twigs and leaves crunched under our feet as we made our way to the entrance, which was just a broken down block of wood which had been placed over the door frame.

We squeezed through the small gap between the wood and the door frame as we stepped foot inside the abandoned building. Particles of dust were visible as the sun shon through small cracks, the sunlight luckily lit the place up more than our flash lights did the first time we visited.

"Why did we run here?" Beau finally questioned as we stepped further into the building.

"I asked someone if they had seen Jai and she said he went into her shop then ran here." I muttered slightly as my eyes scanned our surroundings. Everything looked exactly the same as it did when we first visited, patient records were still scattered across the floors along with old medical tools ect.

"Jai! It's me and Luke!" Beau shouted, his voice echoed throughout the building. I slapped his arm slightly, the last thing we wanted to do was scare him. According to the old woman, Jai thought that there were people after him, I didn't want Beau to startle him anymore.

"Shut up! You'll scare him!" I hissed through my teeth. Beau rubbed his arm softly before turning away.

"We should split up and look for him." I sighed as I gently kicked some of the rubble around as he walked through the hallway. This place was three stories tall and not to mention the amount of rooms. it would take us forever to find Jai if we didn't split up. Though judging by Beau's facial expression, he seemed uneasy by my idea. I knew he was worried something might happen.

"Just call me if something happens." He sighed softly before pulling me into a side hug, patting my back. I nodded before taking off down the hallway to the staircase that led to the second floor. The last time we were here, James and I almost fell to our death when the staircase leading to the third floor collapsed, but lucky enough there were metal staircases for every floor for fire escapes.

My feet pounded up the steps, the metal clunking beneath me as I used the railings to pull myself up quicker.

The place also looked exactly the same, same papers and same medical tools, nothing had been touched. The windows on the second floor were a lot bigger which allowed a lot more sunlight to shine into the rooms.

"Jai? Are you here?" I whispered, I didn't want him to be afraid of me. I ran my hand along the desk that was placed in the middle of the hallway, I could feel the dust from the wood latching onto the bottom of my hand. Opening one of the doors of the desk, a pile of extremely old newspapers fell out on to the floor with a thud, scaring me slightly.

-

"Jai, you don't have to be scared, it's me." I called out quietly, I had by searching the second floor for about ten minutes now with out any sign or clue of Jai even being here. I stepped into one of the patient rooms, the light blue wallpaper was pealing off of the walls, the window had been smashed and the shards of glass were scattered across the floor, the bed now only consist of a small metal bed frame. It was horrifying.

I felt frustrated, frustrated that he was nowhere to be seen. I had promised myself that I wouldn't leave without Jai, and I wanted to keep that promise but I don't know if I could. The little bit of hope I had left slowly began to drain with every empty room I searched.

"Please Jai." I whispered as tears began to sting my eyes, I had to be strong but it was difficult.

Walking out of the room and into the next, I spotted something at the end of the hallway that caught my eye. It looked familiar. I darted down the hallway, the closer I got the more I recognised it. Jai's beanie.

I swiped the beanie up off of floor, holding it tightly in my grasp. Jai had to be here! His beanie was still here! And smile slowly began to tug at my lips, maybe I hadn't found Jai yet but it was still something.

I clutched the beanie close to me, this was what was wearing the night he went missing, I knew he treasured the beanie so it did puzzle me slightly as to why it was just left on the floor. He loved this beanie, my mind began to wander back to the familiar memory.

-

"Jai! I have one more present for you." I called out from our shared bedroom. It was Jai and I's thirteenth birthday and even though we had already exchanged gifts, I wanted to give him something else. I finished wrapping up the gift as I taped down the wrapping paper, my wrapping sucked but it was the thought that counts.

I heard him running down the corridor and into our bedroom, he still had his pajamas on. Mum had said we could sleep in and enjoy the morning and then we would be venturing out with our family and friends for a celebration.

"Luke! You didn't have to get me so many things!" He beamed with an excited smile, we had agreed to get each other a fair amount of gifts but this last one was special.

"Just shut up and open it." I chuckled before tossing him the badly wrapped present. He teared at the wrapping paper, throwing it onto the floor as he held the gift with big eyes.

"Your beanie? Luke you love this thing, I can't take it." He held the beanie out for me, but I pushed it back into his chest slightly. I had bought the beanie on our first trip to America when we were young, even though it was my beanie, Jai loved it just as much as I did and would always pester me for it. I allowed him to wear it but now I wanted him to have it.

"I want you to have it Jai." I chuckled softly. He smiled big at me before fixing the beanie onto his head.

-

I was pulled out of my thought by a warm, wet liquid seeping out of the beanie and onto my hand. I dropped the beanie in shock as I examined my hand, thick red blood had be smeared across my hand from Jai's beanie.

My hands shook uncontrollably as I carefully picked up the beanie, it was soaked with blood.

Chapter Seven

L uke's POV

"BEAU!" My voice echoed with a piercing shriek as the blood continued to seep out of the beanie onto my hands. I was almost positive it was Jai's blood, as much as I didn't want to believe it. Who else's could it be?

Despite the blood oozing out of the cotton, my grip remained tight around the beanie. I was petrified, petrified that something terrible had happened, petrified that I'd never see Jai again.

I began to dash frantically down the hallway, stumbling over the debris that laid around. We needed to get his beanie to the police as soon as possible, it was evidence of some sort. I knew it would be difficult to hand the beanie over to the police since it was Jai's favourite but if it meant helping them find him then I was willing to do it.

"BEAU! QUICK!" My voice sounded like nails dragging along a chalk board, the amount of fear and worry in my voice was obvious. I picked up my speed as I jumped over different objects such as broken chairs and stretchers, I wasn't allowing anything or anyone to get in my way.

"Luke?" I hear Beau's familiar voice shout from the end of the hallway, he had heard my cries and made his way up to the second floor. I had almost made it to him when my foot got caught in the piece of rubble, sending me flying to the floor with a harsh thump. I could physically feel the wind being knocked out of me as my body collided with the ground.

"Luke! Are you okay?!" Beau yelled as he began running towards me, worry evident in his features. I felt a sharp pain in my side as I carefully shuffled around into sitting position.

"Luke, you're bleeding." He whispered as he crouched down to my level. I gently lifted my shirt to see a slight piece of glass imbedded into my side. It was nothing serious but I'd probably use some medical tape to keep the wound clean. Without a second thought, I ripped the piece of glass out with one quick motion, I hissed in pain as the wound began to throb.

"Are you okay?" Beau sighed softly as he helped me back onto my feet. I shook my head in response as I handed him the beanie, his eyes instantly widening at my bloody hands.

"Is this Jai's?" He questioned quietly as held the beanie, careful not to get any blood on his hands.

I trembled violently as my brain tried to piece a sentence together, which was almost impossible. It was if every time I tried to speak my words would just jumble up. Beau soon realised that the beanie was indeed Jai's. I could see the look of fear and sadness instantly wash over his eyes.

This beanie could be last thing left of Jai, I knew thinking like this wasn't going to make the situation any easier, but I couldn't think straight, the many emotions had just gone straight to my head.

"Luke, calm down." Beau instructed as he gently placed his hand on my shoulder, but instead of feeling comforted, I felt angered. How dare he tell me to calm down, our brother is missing and I had just found his beanie drenched in blood! How can I calm down!

I roughly shoved his hand away from my shoulder, stepping away from him. "How can you tell me to calm down?!." I hissed through gritted teeth, though my anger didn't seem to faze Beau one bit.

He carefully placed Jai's beanie to the side before pulling me into his chest tightly. My body trembled as I tried to fight against his grip.

"Please Beau!" My voice cracked as a wave of sadness suddenly over took my anger, my heart instantly sunk into my stomach as the tears rolled down my cheek. I soon enough gave into Beau's strong grip, letting my body relax as I sobbed into his shirt.

He didn't say anything, he remained quiet as he let me cry.

"I need him to be okay!" I screamed through my tears, frustrating getting the best of me. Beau remained silent, rubbing my back soothingly.

"I need you to be strong, strong for Jai okay? We need to go home to mum so we can take his beanie to the police station." He pulled me away from his chest, his hands resting on my shoulders. I hiccuped a few times as I slowly calmed myself down, catching my breath.

"Can you do that?" He questioned, his hands remained on my shoulders. That's what I admired about Beau, he was always so strong even in terrifying situations. I knew he was hurting inside but he put up a brave front to keep me strong.

I responded with a slight nod and a sniffle. He smiled a reassuring smile before carefully helping me up, retrieving the beanie as well.

We carefully climbed over the endless amount of rubble before stumbling through the hallways.

-

Beau and I roughly piled into his jeep, terror running through our veins. After discovering Jai's beanie. We had searched the building on our way out for anymore clues, the only clue was the blood soaked in Jai's beanie, other than that there was no evidence of him being there.

I held his beanie close to me, blood was still seeping out of the cotton and onto my hands but I couldn't care less, we just needed to get this beanie to a police station.

I prayed and prayed that the blood didn't belong to Jai, though it was likely it was his. I mean it's his beanie, his beanie that is drenched in blood. Tears stung my eyes as they effortlessly rolled down my cheeks, landing into my lap.

This wasn't supposed to happen, it was supposed to be a fun night out, filming spooky things for the fans. We were all supposed to return home and watch horror movies until our eyes couldn't stay open, we were supposed to shovel down bowls of popcorn whilst we watched the movies. Jai wasn't supposed to go missing, we weren't supposed to find his beanie covered in blood a day later.

I choked on a sob as I held his beanie close to me, gently resting my head against the car window as the scenery passed by as a blur. This was all one big mistake, it was a stupid idea and now Jai is the one paying for it. I couldn't imagine how scared he must be, all alone in a strange town, I didn't even know if he was still alive!

I tried my best to remain strong for Jai, but the emotions were overwhelming to the point that I couldn't control them.

Beau patted my thigh gently, failing to say a thing. I knew he couldn't find the words to comfort me, he was going through the same pain.

The hour drive home was filled with silence, though the air was full of fear and panic. My heart was pounding like a drum against my chest, almost audible. Beau's fingers gripped the steering wheel, his knuckles turning white. I knew how guilty Beau felt, it was his idea for us to visit the asylum, but the intended trip was supposed to be fun. I kept trying to convince him that it wasn't his fault but my attempts failed.

-

We pulled into our small drive way, the rocks crumbling under the cars tyres. We didn't waste a second to unbuckle our belts and run into the house. But due to my desperation to get this beanie to mum so we could take it to the police station, I had failed to notice the police vehicle already parked outside our house.

Beau slammed the front door open, almost knocking it off its hinges. Mum was sat on the sofa, her head in her hands as her body jerked slightly, it was obvious she was crying. Two police men in uniform say opposite her with a pencil and a note pad, a sympathetic look on their faces.

Noticing our presence, one officer stood up to greet us.

"Boys, I'm officer Dean, I'm here to investigate the disappearance of Jai Brooks." He announced in a strict voice. Hearing those words exit his mouth tore violently at my heart strings.

Before Beau had the chance to respond to officer Dean, I gently pushed him aside, holding up Jai's beanie. "I found Jai's beanie at the place he went missing." My voice came out quiet, I didn't care how weak I sounded.

My mothers head shot up at my words, her eyes widening at the sight of Jai's beanie covered in blood. Her body shook violently as she cried. "My baby!" She sobbed, gasping for air. Beau hurried to her side to comfort her the best he could.

Officer Dean pulled out a pair of latex gloves from his pocket, slipping his hands into them before he took the beanie from me. The blood smudged into his gloves as he carefully examined it, his lips fell into a straight line as he pulled a small clear evidence bag from his pocket, carefully placing the beanie inside of it.

"The item will be taken to the station where an examination will be carried out as soon as possible to identify the blood." He stated.

I didn't want him to take the beanie, but I knew that for Jai's sake, I had to let him. This could be a major clue in finding Jai, and I wasn't just gonna throw it away just because I wanted to keep the beanie close to me.

"Your mother here has given us Jaidon's details, we will file a missing persons report and launch an investigation, we'll have detectives searching this location and the location at which he disappeared." Officer Dean informed us.

I felt a somewhat sense of relief, hopefully the investigation will lead to clues as to what happened that night and I pray that it will only end in happiness. I pray that we will find Jai safely and bring him home where he belongs, with his family.

What do you think happened to Jai? Are you guys enjoying this story?

Chapter Seven: Part Two.

- -

Third Persons POV.

The small four walls held darkness, a cold breeze seeping in through the slight cracks that had formed in the wooden walls over the years. The floor was damp, grass and leaves had grown between the broken floor boards.

The four walls were vandalised, symbols covering every inch and every corner of the small broken hut. Spider webs had formed in the corners, different insects nesting in every place possible.

And in the left corner, a boy sat shaking, his knees pulled into his chest whilst his arms hugged them, desperate for warmth. His clothes were ripped, covered in mud and blood, his curly brunette hair had been matted down to his head and his hazel eyes now dull and lifeless.

Cuts were visible along his knuckles as he tightly gripped onto what was left of his trousers, he rocked himself back and forth in a slow manner, his gazed fixed on the floor in front of him.

"I don't want to die." He whispered to himself.

Not really a chapter but more of a filler! After the idea was suggested I thought that you guys should get a little peek from someone else's POV other than Luke's just to keep the story more interesting.

Chapter Eight

L uke's POV

"Have the police tested the blood yet?" I eagerly questioned my mum, she had wrapped herself up in her dressing gown as she poured herself a cup of tea. She had been taking time off of work and had allowed Beau and I to miss school for a few days.

"Luke, it's been an hour since they left, I told you I'd let you know as soon as I know anything." She sighed heavily before rubbing her hand across her forehead. I felt bad, I had probably asked the same question about 50 times in the last hour.

Mum had not slept at all either, she had huge backs under her eyes and her face had lost its colour. Beau was the only one remaining strong.

I remained silent, a sudden idea popping into my head. I eagerly raced into my bedroom, slamming the door shut behind me. I pulled my back pack out of the closet, retrieving my camera.

I had had the camera on record the entire time we had visited the asylum, this could hold answers!

I switched the camera on with a click before setting up my laptop, whilst giving the laptop time to load I fetched the connecting wire from the drawer, plugging one end into the camera and the other into the laptop.

The fact that I was recording that night had completely slipped my mind, I had been so worried and stressed out that I'm pretty sure I could be forgotten my own name. I prayed that something would show up on the camera, just anything that could give us information!

I pressed settings with a click of a button before allowing the camera and computer to connect to each other.

A familiar swarm of butterflies began forming in the pit of my stomach as the video loaded, I was scared but I needed to know. He couldn't just vanish without a trace, it should be impossible to just completely disappear like that.

My hands shook as the mouse hovered over the play button, debating whether or not I should click the button.

Sucking in a deep breath through my nose, I sat down in the computer chair before plucking up the courage to press play. I held my breath as the video began playing.

The screen showed the five of us, introduced ourselves as we usually do before we began entering the building. Nothing out of the ordinary.

The screen showed the amount of rubble and trashed equipment that had been abandoned, our laughs and conversations were audible as the video progressed. Again, nothing out of the ordinary.

I let go of the breath I was holding as nothing unusual showed up, I leaned back into the chair, my eyes glued to the computer screen as I watched every movement and listened to every word. Laughter filled my ears as the camera focuses on Jai's face, a huge smile spread across his lips as he laughed. The sight made my heart swell with sadness, I needed him home more than ever. He had to be okay.

The video continued, I had captured the moment that Jai had decided to prank us all, a small smile tugging at my lips as I remembered a similar prank Jai had decided to pull on me when we were six years old.

-

"Jai! Look at this cool toy I got!" My six year old self yelled obnoxiously at the top of my lungs. I had just found a super cool race car that had been left at the park. It was only small, it had been painted red with a white stripe down the middle. I couldn't wait to show Jai!

"Jai?" I questioned loudly, receiving no response. I saw my mother in the kitchen chopping up differ not vegetables.

"Mummy, where's Jai? I need to show him this car!" I asked, holding the little car high up in the air. She shook her head slightly as a smile formed on her lips. "I don't know baby, you'll have to find him!" She playfully shrugged.

Before I could continue searching, my mother placed the kitchen knife onto the counter before crouching down to my level.

"Here's a hint though, I think I heard him you guys' room." She winked, poking my nose playfully.

A huge grin formed on my face as I took off down the corridor and into our bedroom. "Oh Jai? Where are you?" I sang. I saw something bulging from under his bed sheets, it had to be him!

I tip toed towards his bed. "Gotcha!" I squealed as I roughly ripped the sheets off of his bed but it had only revealed a few pillows. "Oh." I grumbled.

I know where he is! He must be in the closet! As I was about to turn around I felt a pair of warm hands gently grasp my shoulders, shaking me slightly. "BOO!" The familiar voice boomed. I jumped at the sudden contact, seeing Jai clutching his stomach with laughter which soon encouraged me to laugh along with him.

-

I smiled sadly as the memory played through my brain, my eyes prickling with the familiar sensation as the tears ran freely down my cheeks. I missed him more than anything.

Snuffling slightly, I used the end of my sleeve to wipe my eyes dry when suddenly something on the screen caught my eyes. My heart practically stopped, my blood turned cold and my stomach churned painfully.

"Oh my god." I whispered with wide eyes, replaying the scene over and over.

Chapter Nine

- -

Third Persons POV.

His frail body shook violently in the far corner, his arms wrapped weakly around his legs as he embraced himself with as much strength as he could possibly gather.

A bitter cold gust of wind seeped through the wooden walls that surrounded him, tickling at his skin causing a layer of goosebumps to form. His teeth chattered together slightly as his body desperately tried to provide him with the slightest bit of warmth. But he was helpless.

His eyes, which were previously a vibrate hazel had transformed into nothing but a dull shade. His once smooth olive skin had visually deteriorated to a ghostly pale white, purple and blue bruises decorated different areas of his body.

He gently rocked himself back and forth, he had been surrounded by the darkness for two days now.

His stomach growled in hunger, longing for foods or liquids which he had been deprived of for two days, the effects taking toll as his bones ever so slowly became more visible.

Suddenly, a figure began manifesting in the centre of the little hut, a figure that the boy had the unfortunate luck of becoming familiar with. His eyes widened in terror as the dark figure had manifested to its full form.

"S-stay away." Jai whispered, his voice sounded husky but quiet due to the lack of communication. He desperately began to push his body as far into the corner as he possibly could, eager to escape the figure.

The figure remained silent as it stood tauntingly in the centre of the hut, the figure was beginning to feed from the fear that was radiating from Jai's body, giving it energy.

"P-please!" Jai screeched, his voice sounding like nails dragging roughly down a chalk board.

Without any warning, a large muscular hand roughly clamped itself around Jai's mouth. Instantly, he began struggling against the hand as his arms shot in every direction, his legs kicking out in hopes to kick whoever it was away with him. But his desperate attempts failed him as his kicks and punches connected with nothing but thin air.

His eyes squeezed shut tightly, the hand covering his mouth was preventing Jai from receiving any oxygen. His actions slowly became weaker and weaker as the hand remained in place. Jai's screams for help muffled.

His eyes began feeling heavier as his head felt lighter, his arms fell weakly by his sides as his head fell back against the wall. The little bit of energy left in him slowly vanishing.

Chapter 10

Luke's POV.

It had been an entire week since Jai's disappearance and an entire week of misery and sadness for me. I still hadn't wrapped my head around the fact that my brothers face was now on a missing persons report.

The police still hadn't contacted us with results about the blooded beanie, so I still had no clue whether the blood was his. A huge chunk of me believed it was his blood since it was his beanie, but a little piece of me wanted to believe that it wasn't.

Beau and I had pretty much been sulking around the house for the past week, we hadn't left the house at all since we discovered the beanie. We slowly came to realisation that there was nothing we could do to help the investigation. I hadn't told the police about the text Jai's phone received on the night he went missing either, they'd probably think I was going insane, I know that Beau did.

Today I would be attending school again, despite all of my pleas, my mum insisted that it would be good for me. She told me that sitting at home would be a constant reminder of what happened since I didn't have anything occupy my mind.

Kicking the wrinkled bed sheet covers from my body, I climbed down the ladder and onto the floor, the cool air instantly hitting my skin. I peaked into Jai's bunk, seeing nothing but a messy bed. Seeing his bed empty every morning made my heart ache terribly, he needed to be home safe and warm.

I blinked back the burning sensation that soon began to fill my eyes, I had been like this everyday since he went missing. Having to fight the urge to break down every morning.

I sloppily exited the bedroom before dragging myself down the hall and into the small bathroom. I was instantly faced with my reflection and boy did I look awful. My hair was a matted mess on top of my head, my eyes were blood shot and tired and the giant bags under my eyes made me look a thousand times worse. I looked dead, I had practically lost the will to live.

The tap turned on with a squeak as I let the warm water spill into my hands, it eased me slightly. I splashed a handful of the warm water onto my face, I didn't have the energy to wash my face with soap. I continued on with my usual bathroom routine which consisted with brushing my teeth and styling my hair to be somewhat more presentable.

But unfortunately, the sleepless nights had took its toll.

Exiting the bathroom, in the corner of my vision I could see my mother slouched over the oven cooking eggs. Even with the recent events, she still continued remain as strong as possible for me and Beau which I was entirely grateful for.

As I slumped down the hall lost in a trail of thought, I was met with a hard thump, causing me to stumble slightly. Groaning as I rubbed my chest slightly, Beau was stood in front of me half asleep. His hair was pointing in almost every direction and his eyes were droopy, I chuckled lightly as he simply yawned and continued walking without a word.

-

"Are you sure I have to go?" I questioned my mum with big eyes, she chuckled softly with a sad smile. I knew she only wanted what was best for me but I'd honestly rather be home with my family, not with a bunch of kids I never speak to.

"You'll be fine Luke, it'll help take your mind away from things for a few hours." She replied, carefully straightening out the dreadful uniform we were required to wear.

She pulled me by my shoulders, placing a kiss on my cheek before gently shoving me out of the door. "Now go, have a good day." She chuckled, crossing her arms over her chest. She was still dressed in her pajamas and dressing gown, and I doubt she'd be getting dressed at all today.

A soft sigh escaped my lips but I obeyed her, the school was a short walk from our house which I was thankful for.

The gravel crumbled underneath my feet with each step I took, it was quite chilly out today even though the sun was beaming down on the city. I could feel my nose getting colder and colder every time the wind brush passed me.

I was dreading school, I knew I was going to be asked thousands of questions about Jai, word spreads quick here so the entire school probably knew what happened that night. I wanted to be left alone. The only people I wanted to associate myself with today was James, since he's the only friend I have in this damn school other than Jai.

I heard fast approaching steps, instinctively I whipped my head around seeing none other than the school jock, Jason, running towards me. Gritting my teeth I turned away hoping he'd get the hint.

"Hey Luke! I'm sorry about what happened to your brother." He roughly slammed his hand against my back. He smiled big, his white teeth on display and I couldn't help but want to knock every one of them out. Jason had never acknowledged my presence prior to what happened with Jai, but now my brothers face is all over the news he suddenly noticed my existence.

"Sorry doesn't change anything." I spat rather harshly, I needed to get away from him, I didn't want his attention. As I was about to do so, blue flashing lights suddenly caught my eye. The source of the lights, which happened to be an ambulance and police car, whizzed past me before pulling over into a nearby forest on the opposite side of the road.

I had noticed two police men dressed head to two in paper yellow overalls with a white mask covering their faces, they unraveled a long thin piece of tape before forbidding entrance to the forest.

I stopped dead in my tracks, my heart beating instantly speeding up as one person came to mind. Jai.

Without thinking nor looking I sprinted across the road, I had suddenly forgotten everything and everyone in that moment until I heard Jason's voice scream in terror.

"LUKE WATCH OUT!" His voice rang in my ears but my brain didn't process his words.

My legs froze as a vehicle forcefully hit me at a great amount of speed, my body sent flying through the air before landing painfully in the middle of the road. My vision instantly blurring as people rushed to my side in horror.

Dun dun dunnnnnnn

Chapter 11

Luke's POV

My surroundings were fuzzy but slowly piecing themselves together, though when my vision had restored itself my eyes darted around the room. The familiar red walls covered with posters, the familiar mattress and bed sheets engulfing my body. I was home.

Confusion washed over me as scrambled up into sitting position, my laptop was placed on my lap. Shouldn't my body hurt? Shouldn't I have cuts and bruises? I lifted up the duvet and ran my hands over my stomach, arms and leg but no pain occurred. My breathing became heavier as I gazed at the black screen in front of me, my reflection gazing back.

But not a single scratch. How is that possible?

Quickly switching on the laptop, the screen instantly showed my previous search which was the video from that night.

Then it all clicked in my brain, I was dreaming. They didn't find Jai's body, it wasn't my first day at school and I hadn't been hit by a car, it was all a dream. But unfortunately, Jai's disappearance wasn't a dream. I had fallen asleep after trying to analyse what I had found in the video.

I balled my fists and rubbed my eyes slightly, before pressing play on the video. The images showed on the screen still shooting shivers up my spine.

There on the screen showed Jai stood in the asylum, Beau stood in front of him and James stood beside him, I remember that exact moment. But behind Jai was a dark shadowed mist slowly manifesting into a dark figure before fading away completely.

I slammed the laptop shut roughly, I didn't want to see anymore. It could've just been one of our shadows, I couldn't tell mum or Beau or anyone for that matter, they'd think I'm going insane. Maybe I was?

I sucked in a deep breath before running my hands over my face, my temperature had gone up quite a bit. I needed to get out of the house.

Unwrapping myself from the warmth of my bed sheets, I climbed my way out of the bunk bed. I stood still, debating what to do. I felt lost, I felt empty and I felt alone. I didn't know what to do with myself. I exited the bedroom before making my way towards the bathroom, I needed to freshen up, maybe it'll make me feel better.

Discarding my clothes, I hopped into the shower before turning the tap. The warm droplets of water pounded against my skin but it somewhat relaxed me.

I let the water engulf my body as I stood and thought.

Where was Jai? The question that haunted me the most. I didn't know if he was okay, I didn't know if he was safe. Part of thought that if he was okay then he would've at least tried to find his way home, maybe he got lost on the way? There were endless scenarios to where he was but I needed an answer before the worry ate me alive.

My mind wandered back to the text, a text from Jai's phone to Jai's phone, that shouldn't even be possible!

Before my brain could even process what was happening, dark red liquid began to mix with the water before looking at the bottom of the shower, gasping at the sight I instantly ran my hands frantically over my body, checking for the source.

Nothing.

Glancing up, I screeched in pure horror. The shower head began spitting out droplets of ice cold red liquid. The droplets landed on my skin before rolling off, leaving a trail behind.

Instinctively I began to thrash about, my body tangling with the shower curtain as I desperately began to escape the shower, the red liquid continued seeping from the shower head, drenching my body carelessly.

"HELP!" My voice sounded like sharp nails being dragged down a chalk board.

The temperature of the liquid began to warm up, gradually turning into unbearable heat. The droplets not only stained but scolded my skin every time they came into contact.

The heat caused the bathroom to fog up, the mirrors and Windows had steamed over completely, nothing in the bathroom was entirely visible other than my own body and the gruesome liquid spitting from the shower.

"PLEASE!" I screamed.

The more I thrashed around, the more tangled I became.

I used every bit of energy my body held before throwing myself out of the shower, the curtain remaining wrapped around me. My body collided with the cold hard floor, bringing a sense of relief to my scolded skin.

The shower taps came to a slow stop, the flow of the liquid dripping slightly from the shower head.

My heart was pounding violently against my chest, my throat was dry and I felt extremely light headed from the fear. My hands shook violently as I grabbed the nearest towel, wrapping it tightly around my body.

My skin was red raw from the beat, my legs had slight blistering also. I brought my knees to my chest, hugging them as I sunk into the towel. And sob escaped my lips as I buried my face into my knees, sniffling and sobbing.

Uh oh, what do you think just happened?

Chapter 12

Luke's POV

The remaining water dripped achingly against the shower floor, filling the deathly silence. The cold bathroom tiles numbing my skin, the only warmth my body received was from the pale blue towel wrapped tightly around my shoulders.

My breath hitched as I shakily hauled myself up from the floor, glancing at the shower floor as I did so. Nothing except water, no blood, just water.

Salty tears pooled in my eyes, my bottom lip quivering slightly as my gaze fixated on the shower floor. I can't be going crazy, I saw it with my own eyes. I saw the trails it left behind on my body when the blood pounded against my skin, I saw it!

On time, the wooden bathroom door was harshly kicked open, slamming into the wall, the hand towels which were hung on the door had fallen to the floor.

My eyes met with Beau's piercing green ones, though they didn't hold their usual happiness, instead they were full of worry and concern. His eyebrows knitted together as his eyes darted around the bathroom, scanning it.

"What happened? Why were you screaming?" He questioned, confusion laced within his words.

My mouth gaped open as the salty tears trickled down my cheeks, he was going to think I was insane.

"B-blood." My voice didn't sound the same, it felt like someone had their hands wrapped around my neck, making me choke on my own words. Beau's eyes widened slightly as he continued searching for the source of my screaming.

"Blood? Where? Are you hurt?" He questioned frantically.

My nose felt stuffy, my eyes stung and there was a huge lump wedged in my throat, how am I even supposed to explain what just happened? He'll think that I'm losing my mind, I wanted to lie, tell him that I was alright. But he knew, he knew something was very wrong. And I knew that he would not stop pushing me until I tell him.

"T-the shower." I whispered, my voice cracking with almost every word.

Beau raised an eyebrow, peaking into the shower as he visually examined the shower walls and floor.

"There's no blood there Luke, are you feeling okay?" He gently pressed his hand against my forehead before quickly pulling it back. "You're burning up bro.".

I sniffled softly, wiping away my trail of tears with the back of my hand before shaking my head.

"I need to go." My voice was shaky and weak, I hated feeling weak but at this point I didn't care. I just needed to go. Go somewhere.

"Go wh-" Before Beau even had the chance to finish his sentence, I nudged myself past him and quickly out of the bathroom, the cool air suddenly hit me as I ventured into my bedroom, slamming the door roughly behind me, causing a few items to fall to the ground.

I desperately dried myself off before throwing on any piece of clothing I could find, I didn't care whether my clothes matched of not, I didn't care for people's opinions. I just didn't care about anything.

I pulled a navy blue beanie over my hair before hurrying out of the bedroom.

Beau and mums desperate pleas for me to talk to them echoed through the house, though their words went through one ear and straight out the other. My mind was all over the place.

Ignoring the agony in their voices, I desperately ran out of the house, not bothering to shut the front door behind me. I allowed my legs to carry as fast as they could, wherever they could. My surroundings becoming a blur as I raced down the street, I had no clue where I was going.

The familiar stinging sensation pricked at my eyes again, this was becoming too much for me. I didn't know how to cope. The harsh wind scraped at my cheeks and nose, turning them into a rosy red colour.

My heart ached as images from that night flashed in my mind. How could something so innocent and harmless turn into something so dangerous. My entire heart was beaten to a pulp within seconds, my entire life had been turned upside down in seconds. It's amazing what can go wrong within the span of a few seconds.

I'd never felt so much emotional pain in my life, my heart physically ached for him to return back home safely. The will to live became smaller and smaller every passing day.

I'd never been good with expressing my emotions, I'd usually bottle them up until I couldn't handle it anymore, but this time was different, this time

I wanted to cry, I didn't want to prevent myself from crying because it made me feel worse. I wanted to scream, I wanted to cry and I wanted to punch the nearest object. I wanted someone to blame. And the person I blamed was myself.

Chapter 13

Jai's POV

A month, almost a month. Away from my family for almost a month, starved of real nutrition, without a change of clothes for a month.

My stomach grumbled achingly, the sound had echoed off of the four wooden walls. I hadn't eaten for three days, I hadn't been allowed to eat for three days. He said I didn't deserve food, he said I was being punished. I didn't understand what for, the lack of food and water had taken a huge toll on my body, I was slowly weakening every passing day.

Simple movements were gradually becoming painful, my body clung to whatever energy it was storing. My bones were slowly becoming more visible, poking out from underneath my skin. Though it had only been a month, my body had demanded the food it had been forbidden, and until it got that food, it would soon start attacking itself.

I pulled my knees into my chest, hugging them loosely, it hurt too much. My back pressed against the corner of the wall, the small room was drowned in darkness, nothing or no ones present. I wanted to go home.

My mind failed me, I didn't have the slightest clue how this had happened, how I ended up here. All I remembered was a dark figure, completely dark figure, it appeared to be lacking any facial features. Though I was unsure whether my mind had created this figure due to the lack of food and water, I had lost sense of reality. It was becoming difficult to tell the different between what was real and what was not.

I wanted to cry, but I couldn't produce any tears, I was so dehydrated.

Slowly and shakily, I spread out across the wooden floor, scrunching my nose at the sudden discomfort. The floor was damp, different types of grass and moss had begun growing between the floor boards, attracting insects as well. There was only one window, it had been invaded by moss making it impossible to see out of. I wanted to smash the window, I wanted to escape. But the window was too small for me to fit through.

I had taken off what was left of my shirt, bundling it up before placing it on the floor, resting my head on top of it. My clothes were ripped and tatty, they were covered in dirt. They were ruined and torn apart every time I had gotten punished, every time I had tried to avoid his punches, he'd pull me back by my clothes, ripping them.

I bundled my arms up under my chin, trying to gain as much warmth as possible. The nights were always below freezing, every inch of my body felt like ice, but I was becoming immune to it.

My eyes instantly felt heavy, I couldn't keep them opened for much longer so I didn't bother to fight it. Sleep was my only escape.

-

The sound of the locks on the opposite side of the door snapping woke me with a startle, my head shot up as I scrambled into fetal position, my body instantly shaking. My breath hitched in my throat as the wooden door slowly creaked open, the daylight creeping through the small gap.

He appeared, without a word, pointing a strict finger at me before throwing something into the room. The object shattered as soon as it connected with the floor, though even with the small amount of light peeking through, I still couldn't make out what it was.

Again, without a word, he slowly closed the door, instantly bolting it back up. And once again, I was left alone in silence.

Curiosity got the best of me, I wanted to know when he threw.

The nails that held the floor boards in place dug into my hands and knees as I weakly crawled, my hands swiping the floor as I searched for the object.

I hissed in pain as my hand swiped across a broken piece of what felt like glass, I could instantly feel the warm blood seeping from the wound, but I had worse. I had way worse. I wiped the blood into my pants before gently tapping the ground in search for the rest of the glass.

My fingers came across something smooth, I brought it closer to my face, trying my best to make out what it was, thought the slight scent it gave off didn't take me long to realise that it was a single slice of bread. This was my 'dinner'. And the object that had smashed was a plate.

Hungrily, I shovelled the bread into my mouth, not even taken the time to chew it properly. My body craved food, and this is all I would be getting for today.

This is how it has been, every day, for almost a month. And I slowly but surely, I was losing touch with reality.

Chapter 14

L uke's POV

'Local teenager, Jai Brooks, has been missing for a month. His family reported his disappearance last month after the teen failed to return home after a night out with friends. Over the last month there has only been one reported sighting of the boy which unfortunately lead to no clues to his whereabouts. If you or anyone you know see this boy please contact your local police station with your informations.'

Photos of Jai flashed across the television screen as the news reporter spoke with a very strict tone. My heart dropped into my stomach as the broadcast ended. I knew Jai was missing, but until now, I didn't realise the seriousness of it. I thought that a few posters would just be put up around town, but seeing my brothers disappearance being broadcasted on every news channel around Australia made me sick to my stomach.

I reached for the remote, quickly pressing the off button before angrily throwing the remote to the floor.

I was slowly losing my mind without Jai, I had begun hallucinating, seeing things that weren't there. I had grown a fear of showering ever since the incident, I was terrified that it would happen again, even though it was only my mind messing with me, I was still scared.

I had many unpleasant dreams, I would come close to finding Jai in them, only for something terrible to happen before I had the chance. They occurred almost every night, I would wake up startled and spend many hours trying to calm myself down.

I hadn't told Beau or mum about the hallucinations or dreams, they had enough stress on their plates, I didn't need to add onto that. I knew that they were holding themselves together as much as they could for me, but I knew my mum cried herself to sleep every night and I always hear Beau tossing and turning for hours.

I hoped I would've been able to clear my mind by taking long walks, but my mind would always wander back to Jai. Where he was, how was he and if he was still alive, he wouldn't leave my thoughts.

I hadn't had a good night sleep since Jai left, I'd flick through photos of us and cry for hours before finally falling asleep, only to be awoken by nightmares. I knew Beau thought I was losing my mind, I mean he saw me crying and shaking on the bathroom floor over something that wasn't actually there. Not to forget the text message that had been sent from Jai's phone to Jai's phone, he didn't believe me.

I stood up from the sofa, stretching my limbs. I hadn't left the house for days and I refused to. Mum had phoned in sick for work, they had allowed her to take as much time off as she needed, I was thankful for that, even though I was beginning to push her and Beau away, I still needed them more than ever.

The house was quiet, Beau had locked himself away in his room as usual. He had begin to do that a lot, whenever he felt like crying he'd lock himself away, he wouldn't let me comfort him as he didn't want me to see him cry.

I headed into the kitchen, walking past the mirror as I did so. I caught a slight glimpse at my reflection, I looked awful. The loss of sleep defiantly showed on my features. My hair was a curly mess, my hazel eyes which were once bright were now sad and dull and not to mention how dry and blood shot they had become from the endless amount of crying.

Walking into the kitchen, I saw my mum hovering over the stove in her pale pink dressing gown. She was stirring soup, but her movements were weak and effortless, everything had also taken a huge toll on her as well. She was missing her son.

"Hi mum." I spoke quietly, not wanting to startle her. She turned to face me before shooting me an effortless smile, her face was pale and her eyes were tired. "How are you, sweetheart?" She questioned in a hushed tone. Ever since Jai disappeared, the household had become quiet, no one was enthusiastic, no one was happy.

"Been better." I mumbled, seating myself on the breakfast bar stool before placing my arms on the cold counter, snuggling my face into them.

The smell of the soup filled the kitchen, it smelt delicious. And even though my stomach growled hungrily for the taste of it, I didn't want to eat it. Even though my stomach told me I was hungry, I still felt sick to my stomach. Dinner times weren't the same anymore either, we hadn't eaten together as a family for a month. Mum usually dined in the kitchen by herself, Beau would sprawl out on the sofa and eat and I would lock myself away in my room.

I felt a soft hand run gently through my messy curls, I lifted my head to face my mother who stood besides me with a forced smile. I wanted to comfort her, but I didn't know how. How could I bring comfort to someone else when my entire would was broken as well.

"Do you think he's okay?" My voice cracked slightly, the familiar lump forming in my throat. Mum shifted her weight slightly before letting out a sigh through her nose, her gaze fixated on me.

"I can't answer that Luke, I don't have the answer but I'd like to think he is." She replied, her lower lip trembling slightly as the words exited her mouth.

They weren't the words I wanted to hear, I wanted her to tell me that he was okay, that he'd be home soon. But that wasn't the truth.

"Do you think he'll be found?" I drifted my gaze from hers to the counter, fumbling with my fingers nervously.

"We can't lose faith in him." Was all she said. I knew she didn't want to give me any false hope, so she was always careful with her choice of words.

I bit my bottom lip in prevention of tears, I nodded slightly. This shouldn't of happened, if I could go back to that night and prevent us from going to that asylum then I would've in a heart beat.

I was about to question my mum further, ask her what she thought he was doing right now, but the sound of her mobile phone vibrating interrupted our conversation. She gave me an apologetic smile before placing a loving kiss on my forehead.

"Hello?" She spoke into the phone as she leant against the kitchen counter.

"Yes, this is Gina Brooks." She spoke confidently into the phone, her eyebrows knitting together slightly. I watched her facial features intensely.

"O-oh my god..." Her tone of voice instantly switched from confident to broken within the matter of seconds, her hand shakily shot up to her mouth. My heart beat began to quicken as my mind began to create endlessly scenarios of what the person on the other line was saying.

I quickly stood up from the stool, my breathing becoming heavier as I waited impatiently.

"O-okay t-thank you." She stuttered over her own words, tears had began effortlessly falling down her cheeks as she quickly hung up the phone, placing it back onto the counter.

She steadied her balance by resting both hands against the counter, violent sobs escaping her parted lips.

My heart was breaking. I quickly rushed to her side, pulling her into a gentle hug.

"Mum who was it? What's wrong?!" I questioned, rushing the words out of my mouth. But she didn't answer, she was choking on her sobs.

My mind was playing through different scenarios, was he dead? was he alive? was he hurt?

"Mum please answer me!" I cried frantically, desperate for answers. I placed both of my hands gently against her arms as she looked me in the eye, her nose and eyes were bright read.

She shakily brought her hands to my cheeks, cupping my face gently, a broken expression plastered on her face.

"T-the blood on the beanie was identified as Jai's."

Chapter 15

Beau's POV

I hadn't left my room all day, I'd pretty much locked myself away in here most days. I didn't want mum or Luke to see me weak, I had to be strong for them, for Jai. I had forbidden myself from crying or showing the slightest sign of weakness in front of them. The only time I would ever allow myself to break was when I had locked myself in my room. Like right now.

With the back of my hand, I wiped the warm tears from cheek as I sniffled. It was hard, very hard.

The stronger I remained on the outside, the weaker I became on the inside. I wanted so badly to be comforted, but at the same time I wouldn't allow anyone to see me in this state.

I was scared, scared for Jai. With no idea where he was or how he was, it wasn't easy to rest at all. I couldn't sleep without knowing that he was okay. The night it all happened still remained a blurred mystery to me, I had no clue how it happened or why it happened. And I had no clue whether he was alive or not.

Every night I prayed for him to return home safely, I prayed for our family to be complete once again and I prayed for things to return to how they were. I missed messing with him, I missed teasing him and most of all I missed his warm smile and comforting personality.

I had also become scared for Luke, without Jai he was slowly but surely losing himself. I hear him scream in his sleep every night, he'll cry hysterically over things that aren't actually there, he was losing himself.

A heartbroken cry echoed through the house, pulling me from my trail of thought. Usually I would've been shaken by the sound, but it was slowly becoming all too familiar. The crying and screaming.

I leaped up from my bed after throwing the duvet covers off of myself, racing out of my bedroom and through the hallways. I peaked my head into the living room to see that it was empty.

I heard Luke, his pleading cries echoing through the room. I followed the sound which had lead me to the kitchen.

Luke was sobbing hysterically on the floor, his knees pulled to his chest and he buried his face in them. Mum had her arms wrapped tightly around him, her hand running soothing circles on his back. Tears poured down her cheeks as she gently rocked him, crying quietly as well.

My eyes widened at the sight, worry washing over me intensely. I didn't know what to think, what had happened. I'd seen Luke cry but never like this, he looked torn apart, literally. It pulled at my heart to see him like this.

"What happened?" I whispered, kneeling down besides the two of them.

Mum glanced up at me, her eyes were red shot and puffy, the tip of her nose bright red. She swallowed hard before shaking her head. She opened arm slightly, pulling me into her embrace and she pulled both Luke and I close to her.

"T-the blood was Jai's." She whimpered into my shoulder, her voice was broken.

A huge lump formed in my throat, I felt sick, I felt like was about to throw up any second. My blood turned cold and my heart ached.

Jai was hurt, the blood was his so it was obvious he was hurt. I didn't even know if he was alive but the little hope I clung onto slowly vanished everyday. This shouldn't be happening, not to Jai. Jai didn't deserve this, he's a good kid, what did we do wrong?

"M-mum please call back and double check! There has to be a mistake!" Luke pleaded, his dull hazel eyes practically begging mum. "Please..." He whispered, he was in denial.

Mum shook her head, cupping his face gently as she gazed at him, she held his face tightly, almost as if he were about to disappear.

"I'm so sorry." She whispered, a fresh batch of tears racing down her cheeks and landing onto her lap.

Luke carefully shook himself out of her embrace, a look of anger mixed with sorrow fixed on her. I wanted nothing more to him smile again, it physically pained me to see him like this.

Mum sighed sadly, running her hands over face as she sobbed violently into them. My heart hurting for her. But I promised myself that I'd remain strong.

I carefully pulled her into my arms, allowing her to release all of her emotions as she sobbed. Her tears wetting my shirt but I honestly couldn't care, I was her shoulder to cry on. My eyes prickled with warm tears, everything was slowly becoming overwhelming. Jai was missing and possibly dead, Luke was losing his mind and mum cried herself to sleep every night, it was too much to take in at once.

I was drowning in emotions, but I wouldn't let them see. I needed to be there for them, I needed to be someone they could cry to and I wasn't about to let my feelings get in the way of that.

I bit down hard on my tongue in hope of preventing the tears threatening to fall, there was a huge lump fixed in my throat and it made it hard to stop myself from crying. But I would manage.

"My poor baby." Mum shook as she sobbed, choking on her breath as she gasped slightly. I didn't know what to say, how could I comfort someone when I was feeling the exact same pain.

"He's a fighter mum." Though I didn't know if my words were true. I didn't know it Jai was okay, I didn't know if he would pull through and I didn't even know if he was alive.

She lifted her head up from my chest, the little make up she wore was smudged around her eyes, her cheeks were damp from her endless tears and her nose and eyes were bright red. She smiled at me slightly, a broken smile. "I know he is." She whispered, tears brimming her eyes before effortlessly cascading down her cheeks.

"Everything will be alright."

She didn't reply. I wasn't fooling her and I wasn't fooling myself either, trying to keep a positive mindset was hard but I had to pull through.

I stood up from the floor, carefully helping mum up as well. She brushed off her pale pink dressing gown, before straightening herself up slightly.

She cleared her throat before inhaling a deep breath, drying her eyes slightly. "Go set up the table please, we're eating together today." She ordered quietly before returning to her soup, carefully stirring it.

I nodded, stretching up the the wooden cupboard where all the plates and bowls were stored. The door opened with a squeak. I smiled as I saw a familiar plastic plate, one of Jai's favourite plates as a child, he'd refused to eat dinner if it wasn't served on that red plastic plate.

-

"Dinners ready!" Mums voice chimed through the house, Luke and Jai, who were four, raced into the kitchen, throwing the blocks they had previously been playing with. "Wait for me!" I whined, placing the blocks down. I had been gifted them the day before for my sixth birthday.

My little legs carried me into the kitchen. Luke and Jai both sad at the oak table with their matching aprons. I plopped myself into the wooden chair besides Jai, swinging my legs. "Spaghetti is my favourite!" Luke cheered happily, his eyes lighting up as our mum carefully placed our plates in front of us. "Enjoy!" She grinned before tidying up the cutlery she had used.

Both Luke and I instantly dug into our spaghetti savouring the taste, mum always made the best spaghetti.

"Why aren't you eating, Jai?" Mum questioned, folding up tea towel before neatly putting it away. "I can't eat it." He mumbled quietly, slowly pushing the plate away from him.

"And why can't you eat it?"

"I can't eat food if it's not on my red plate." He whispered, shyly sinking into his seat. Mum chuckled before playfully rolling her eyes, retrieving Jai's spaghetti before dishing it onto his favourite red plate.

"Is that better?" She questioned, but by the way instantly shovelled the food into his mouth gave her her answer. We all broke out into fits of giggles at how fussy he could be.

Tears stung at my eyes at the memory, and all to familiar feeling of sadness washing over me. The things I would do to go back and keep him safe, to make more happy memories with my brothers.

"Beau, are you okay?" I felt my mums comforting hand on my shoulder, I hadn't realised that I was frozen in place, her touch startled me slightly.

"Y-yeah, I'm okay." I nodded, shaking the thoughts from my head. Be strong Beau.

I carefully carried the plates to the dining table, instinctively setting four out, I bit my lip harshly before realising. I picked up the plate, leaving three on the table before placing the other plate back into the cupboard.

"Will you go get Luke please." Mum ordered quietly, I hated how quiet this house had become. Without Jai here, we didn't laugh and we hardly ever engaged into a conversation. It used to be such a happy environment, always joking around, always laughing and always smiling. But without Jai here, that was impossible.

I obeyed my mums orders, exiting the kitchen. I walked through the hallway, glancing at the photos hung on the walls. Most of them were old school photos, then there were family holiday photos. We all looked so happy, my heart longed for us to be a family again.

I reached Luke's bedroom, knocking on the door though the only reply was a loud smash echoing through the room. What the hell. "Luke!" My voice cracked as I yelled, harshly pushing the door open.

He stood with his back pressed firmly against the wall, beads of sweat coating his skin, his eyes and mouth wide open as his body shook. "P-please tell me you can see that..." He whimpered, shakily pointing to his bedroom window.

I slowly altered my gaze to the window, hoping to catch a glimpse of whatever Luke was seeing. But nothing, nothing was there, just the midnight sky.

"There's nothing there bud."

"But there is Beau! Please believe me!" He cried, a look of horror fixed on his face as he continuously gazed at the window.

"Why can't you see it!"

Chapter 16

- -

Beau's POV

I gently placed my hand against Luke's shoulder, I didn't want to startle him. His warm hazel eyes were coated by a layer of tears, all of the colour had pretty much drained from his face leaving his skin a ghostly white. His lips were parted as he gaped at whatever it was he could see. He hadn't moved a muscle for the last few minutes.

I glanced between Luke and the window, but nothing unusual jumped at me, actually nothing at all jumped at me as nothing was there other than the dimmed reflection from the bedroom light.

"Luke bud, I think you need to sleep." I suggested, trying my best to encourage him to at least move.

"N-no Beau, they're going to kill him." He stuttered, his words slightly jumbled. I furrowed my eyes, who's going to kill who? Why did he think this? And most of all, what on earth was he seeing?

"Why would you think that?" I questioned, confusion and worry evident in my tone of voice. I pushed against his shoulder gently, hoping to guide him to the bed so he could sit down but he refused to move a muscle. He was almost in a state of trance, as if he were in a different world.

He shook his head slightly, but he remained still, his eyes glued to the window.

"Why can't you see it." His voice had slowly drained of emotion, the sudden lack of emotion within his facial features and his tone of voice concerned me greatly.

I was beginning to grow frustrated with him, I knew he was mourning for Jai and I knew that the lack of sleep was messing with him, but I couldn't help but feel frustrated, I just wanted to know what the heck was going on inside his head.

"There's nothing there Luke." I groaned in annoyance, I was beginning to think that these little 'episodes' of his were a cry for attention.

He took a few steps forward, standing directly in front of the window. I watched his reflection carefully through the glass, observing his expressions and gestures. He gently glided two fingers along the cold glass, his eyes following them intently as he brought them up in front of his face.

"Now can you see it?" He questioned, his tone of voice sounding dull and bored. He held his fingers up towards me, his eyes glued to them.

Nothing. There was absolutely nothing there, the window and his fingers were both normal.

"I can't see anything Luke." I sighed.

He roughly wiped his fingers along his jeans, wiping whatever he thought was there into the fabric. "You're useless." He spat, harshly pushing passed me with a thud before exiting his room, leaving me in astonishment.

I stood still, shock washing over me. What the hell was that about, one minute he was dazed and out of it and then the next he was angered.

He slammed the bedroom door shut, posters and photo frames jolting slightly. Slowly walking to wards the window, I stared intently at it, hoping to see at least something. But no matter how hard I looked, my eyes just couldn't pick up on anything usual.

This was becoming frustrating, at least once or twice a day Luke would have some weird episode, screaming violently at something that wasn't there or his moods would suddenly switch without any warning.

But no matter how hard I beg him to tell me what he sees, he refuses, there's no budging him. It's like he's in his own little world, completely oblivious to everything and everyone around him for those few minutes.

There was absolutely no point in trying to get through to him when he became like this, everything I or mum would say just went through one ear and straight out of the other. This had only occurred since the day Jai went missing, it started when he had convinced himself that Jai's phone had received a message from Jai's number, which was highly impossible.

My thoughts were interrupted by a thick red substance instantly catching my gaze, my heart beat increased as my brain analysed what it was. A thin trail of dark red liquid was oozing from the window sill, trickling into the floor before making a small trail to the bottom of Jai's bunk.

I slowly bent down, my knees feeling weak as I did so, I didn't dare touch the blood though. I carefully traced the trail of blood, my hand reaching underneath the bed where it lead to. Something thin and cold came into contact with my skin, sending instant shockwaves through my body.

I slightly grasped the object, carefully pulling it from underneath the bed.

Scissors, a pair of scissors coated in the red substances. My hands shook violently as I quickly let them slip from my grasp, hitting the tiled floor.

"Now do you believe me." Luke's voice whispered into my ear.

Short chapter I know! I have loads of ideas for this book so I'm writing them all out for you guys! :)

Chapter 17

B eau's POV

Mum, Luke and I silently gathered around the kitchen table, the soup mum had prepared for us had unfortunately turned cold so she allowed us to order food in since she wasn't in the mood or state of mind to cook anything else.

Mum had heard the chaos between Luke and I when I had discovered the bloody scissors and the look on her face when she caught a quick glimpse of them was pure horror.

She had taken the scissors and kept them on a dry paper towel, I knew she wanted to inform the police of our findings but first she had sat us around the table for a talk.

"Luke, why didn't you tell anyone about the scissors underneath Jai's bed?" She questioned sternly, her tired eyes boring into his.

Luke shuffled uncomfortable in his seat, running a hand through his curls before signing softly. "I didn't know they were there."

For some reason, I didn't believe him. I knew Luke wouldn't give into mums questions anyway and I knew that sooner or later mum would grow frustrated and this whole little meeting would end up with us shouting and screaming.

"Then what were you so scared of when I found you screaming at absolute nothing?" I hissed, nudging his leg slightly. I didn't mean lose my temper with him but over the past month all of my unreleased emotions were finally getting the best of me, and Luke being so secretive of what he was seeing wasn't making things any easier.

"Calm down Beau." Mum sighed softly, gently rubbing her hand over my back which somewhat eased me slightly.

"Why won't you tell us what's going on in your head Luke? Don't shut us out." Mum begged, her voice was fill with various emotions. Sadness, frustration, concern ect.

Luke ran his hands over his face, covering his eyes as he rested his head in his hands. He bit roughly at his bottom lip, tugging at his black lip ring. "Because you'll think I'm crazy." He whispered.

He sounded truly broken and scared, and as much frustration he brought to me, I couldn't help but feel terrible for him. He was missing his twin and I was being insensitive for letting my anger out on him.

"We won't think you're crazy, we just want to be there for you." I stated.

"And we can't be there for you if you shut us out." Mum added, to which I nodded in agreement.

He sniffled slightly, it didn't take long for me to figure out that he was crying quietly. Tears cascading down his pale cheeks as he hid his face in his hands, almost as if he were ashamed of his emotions. "I've just been hallucinating, that's all."

Both mum and I sighed softly, knowing it would take a little while for him to tell us exactly what he has been seeing. The room was dead silent, you could almost hear a pin drop. When Jai disappeared, he took all the happiness and laughter with him, we weren't complete without him here.

"I'm going to ask you again, do you know where the scissors came from?" Mum pushed, her tone of voice becoming stern. Being soft with him wasn't going to get him to tell us, we had to push him.

He inhaled a deep breath, raising his head from his hands before staring mum dead in the eye. "No, I don't." He shook his head.

Mum just nodded, staring at the pair of scissors that were placed securely on the counter.

"Please tell me Luke, if you didn't know the scissors were there then what did you see?" I practically pleaded, I was desperate to know what was going on inside his head and I know that mum was too.

I watched him carefully, he body posture slouching into his seat as his hands fiddled with the ends of his grey hoodie. His eyes were glued to his fingers as he stared at them intently, I could tell he was thinking.

"I-I saw blood." He whispered quietly, avoiding eye contact.

Mum and I glanced a each other, a look of hope fixed on our faces as Luke finally opened up, even if it was only a little bit. It was something.

"Blood?" I questioned.

"Yes."

He continued to fiddle with ends of his sleeves, still avoiding eye contact with both mum and I. He wetted his lips slightly as he took a shaky breath. I gently placed my hand against his back, letting him know that it was okay.

"T-there were weird s-symbols written with b-blood." His voice was extremely quiet, he sounded ashamed and scared.

Mums gaze lowered to the table as she thought, her expression was sad, I knew she wanted to help him but there was only so much that we could do.

"Why didn't you tell us?" Mum sighed softly, standing up from her chair, the legs of the chair squeaking against the floor as she did so. She embraced Luke into a warm loving hug.

"Because you'd think I'm crazy." He whimpered, hiding his face.

Mum shook her head, her eyes filling with tears as a sad smile spread across her lips. "I don't think your crazy, I think you're scared and you're mind is playing games with you, the lack of sleep is catching up with you bud." She sighed, running a hand through his curls.

I agreed with her, he hadn't had a good nights sleep for months, neither of us had, but Luke seemed to have taken the situation a lot worse, which was completely understandable.

"I'm going to take the scissors down to the police station." She stated, placing a kiss on Luke and I's foreheads before carefully taking the scissors into her hands.

"W-wait what? I-is that necessary?" Luke nervously stuttered, shooting us from his seat. I raised an eyebrow at his sudden nervousness.

His slowly cowered into the corner of the room, his hands shaking slightly as his hazel eyes widened. His suddenly behaviour worried me a lot, he looked as if he were hiding something.

"Yes of course it's necessary." Mum furrowed her eyebrows, also concerned.

He gulped hard before shaking his head, standing in front of the door frame, blocking mum from leaving the room. I instantly stood up, towering over him as I gave him a look that said 'spill it'. His eyes rapidly glanced between both mum and I as he processed his next words.

"Y-you can't give them to the police!" He stuttered, his breathing had become heavy.

"And why can't she?" I lowered my voice in hopes to sound threatening.

There was a long pause, silence once again filling the room. Mine and my mums gaze was fixed on Luke as we watched him stutter and shake nervously. His eyes darted across the room nervously as he thought of the words to say, he was taking heavy breaths. He eventually collapsed, throwing himself to the floor before pulling at his hair harshly.

"I put them there!".

I love leaving you guys hanging ;)

Feed Back

Hey guys, I was just wondering if you could leave your opinions/thoughts on this book in the comments, let me know what you think about it, what you like about it and whatever else you'd like to add. Thank you guys so much for the support!

Chapter 18

B eau's POV

My eyes grew wide as the words left Luke's mouth, silencing everyone. He put the scissors there, I couldn't believe that my own brother would even think of pulling a stunt like this during our situation.

Luke sat slouched on the floor, his body shaking as sobs erupted from him, but this time I didn't feel sympathy, I felt anger. My blood boiled and my body temperature instantly raised. Mum rested herself against the kitchen counter, tears silently falling along her cheeks as she quickly rubbed them away. None of us consoled Luke, what he did was stupid and he didn't need to be comforted for it.

My anger got the best of me, my eyes coated over as I let my actions control me. I harshly yanked Luke up from the floor by the collar of his shirt, my fists turning white as my grip on his shirt tightened. He gasped at the sudden movement, I had obviously taken him by surprise.

"I swear to god, you better not have hurt Jai." I hissed through gritted teeth.

"W-what? N-no! I would never!" His eyes instantly widened at my statement as he shook his head frantically.

"Beau! Calm down." Mum suddenly soothed, carefully pulling me away from Luke but before I had managed to let go of his collar, I pushed him to the ground with a harsh thud. Mum seemed shocked by my sudden actions, but she kept herself quiet.

Part of me felt guilty for lashing out Luke but another part of me didn't, what he did was extremely wrong, planting fake evidence purposely. If mum hadn't confronted both Luke and I and went straight ahead with taking the scissors to the police station then Luke would've landed himself in serious trouble.

I didn't help Luke up, neither did mum, I knew she was extremely upset and disappointed in him as any mother would be.

Luke shuffled himself to sit against the kitchen wall, bringing his knees up to hug his chest as he sobbed quietly. He hadn't even apologised yet and for some reason it added fuel to my fire.

"Don't sit there and feel sorry for yourself." I spat harshly, taking a few steps forward as I towered over him. My eyes burned holes into his as he starred up at me, his eyes blood shot and puffy. He remained quiet as he hugged his knees tightly, sniffling every once in a while, but for some reason, it made me angrier. He was playing victim when he was the one who planted the fake evidence.

"You think it was funny to pull something like that?" I gritted my teeth tightly, my words sounded harsh but frankly I couldn't care less.

I was waiting for mums soft voice to fill my ears, to tell me to stop and leave him alone, but I didn't hear those words. She stood back a quietly cried, this was Luke's fault.

Slowly kneeling down to Luke's level, my gaze complete focused on him. I could tell by his constant fidgeting that it was beginning to make him uncomfortable, but was I going to stop? No.

"It should of been you." My voice was low but my words were audible, Luke's eyes widened in shock and sadness, his bottom lip quivering slightly. But I didn't care, my anger had completely taken over me. "It should've been you!" I repeated myself, raising my voice which had made him jump at my sudden tone.

Before I could get an understanding on what was happening, my fist collided harshly with Luke's cheek, a sickening sound echoing through the kitchen as my fist connected with his cheek.

"Beau!" My mother screeched, I felt her hands roughly grab my shoulders as she quickly pulled me away from Luke, preventing me from doing anything else.

I could see the fear in Luke's eyes, his hands were cupping his cheek as he sobbed uncontrollably. Everyone was in shock, including myself. I had never hit any of my brothers, I'd never brought pain upon them, never.

I sat back in shock, gazing down at my fist. I never meant to hit him, I don't even what possessed me to hit him. I shifted my gaze back to Luke, he quickly shuffled as far away from me as he could, afraid I'd hit him again. This wasn't supposed to happen.

"Beau Brooks you are gr-." Before mum had the chance to finish her sentence, Luke pulled himself up from the floor, his hand still cupping his cheek which was slowly beginning to bruise. His eyes were full of many emotions, sadness, pain ect. His shook slightly, his knees wobbling beneath him as tears cascaded down his cheeks.

"I hid it there because I knew you'd find it, I wanted you to think that you could see the same things I was seeing so you wouldn't think I was crazy, I covered the scissors in fake blood, I didn't want to be the only person seeing those things so I wanted to trick you into thinking you could see them too." He whispered sadly before exiting the kitchen, leaving me and mum drowning in silence.

Chapter 19

Jai's POV

I'd lost count, I'd lost count of how many times I had been beaten, how many times I had been rejected food and water and I had lost count how long I'd been here. I knew it had been a few months, the changing seasons gave that away, I knew I had been away from my family for a long time.

I'd grown so weak, my bones were literally poking out from under my pale skin, it had become a challenge just to lift my arms without feeling tired. Every part of me had become extremely sore to touch.

My eyes felt dry, my stomach was empty, my throat was dry, my legs were weak and just the simplest of movements would cause excruciating pain. Though the person behind all of this didn't think I had endured enough. Every night he'd beat me until I cried myself to sleep, though I couldn't even produce tears, I had become so dehydrated.

I had only been fed a piece of bread and dirty water every other day, he told me I didn't deserve to eat a nice warm meal. Though I was extremely grateful for just a single slice of bread, it gave me that tiny burst of energy.

The nights had become extremely cold as winter was slowly approaching, this little cabin did not provide me enough heat so I was forced to cling onto the little clothing I had left. The wooden walls had become extremely damp and mouldy from the heavy rain that beat down on me every night, the little holes in the wooden roof did not provide me enough shelter to keep me dry.

The poor weather plus lack of food had made me extremely ill, he knew that, but he didn't care.

I hadn't had a decent sleep or shower in many months, my skin was pale and dirty from sleeping in the rotten floor. I had bug bites all over my legs from the tiny insects that would creep into the cabin at night. My clothes weren't even clothes anymore, they had been torn to shreds and dirtied by the endless beatings I'd receive everyday.

I'd save the little bit of dirty water I had been given to drink to use to wash myself as much as I could, but it was pretty much useless.

My stomach cried for a real meal every night but it was never provided with that luxury, as much as I was grateful for the single slice of bread, I knew I couldn't survive much longer without a warm meal or clean water.

But I had some hope that this would be over soon, I'd dream of police pilling up outside the cabin to my rescue. But with every passing day my dream only began to fade.

I had been pulled out my thoughts by the familiar dark figure standing tall over me, he wore a dark outfit that covered his entire body, including his face, which only made him 100 times more intimidating.

My body shook in complete fear as he towered over me confidently, I couldn't see his facial features but I knew he was smirking evilly.

"Stand up." His voice was deep, he had some type of device that disguised his voice, he was extremely smart.

I gulped nervously, he knew I couldn't stand up, I was far to weak, he would use this as another excuse to punish me. I slowly pressed my hands against the damp flooring, gathering up as much energy and strength I could find to help heave my body up, but the second I put weight onto my hands an extremely excruciating pain shot through my body, causing me to yelp out.

The man shook his head disapprovingly, he pulled his foot back, kicking me harshly in my side as i cried out in agony. But he did not show any sympathy or any signs of stopping.

He pulled me harshly by what was left of my tatty shirt, ripping another hole into it during the process, he was so much stronger than I was, my feet were barley touching the ground as he pulled me close to his masked face.

"You will do what I say." He spat, pushing me back to the wet floor board with a thud. As soon as my body connecting with the floor I let out a piecing scream, the force of the impact had definitely broken something and the intense pain that shot through my left arm confirmed that theory.

I rolled onto my side weakly, hugging my broken arm close to my chest to bring some kind of comfort, but it was useless.

He crouched down to my level, gently taking my broken arm in his hands. I wanted to pull away, but I knew that this would end up with me being severely punished even more. His touch was gentle this time, his gloved hands traced soft lines up and down my broken arm.

I watched him carefully, though I couldn't see his facial features or emotions, I desperately hoped he had realised what he had done was wrong.

But in this situation, I was wrong.

Before I even had the chance to move my broken arm away from his gentle grasp, his free hand had been lifted high into the air before connecting harshly with my arm, a sickening crack echoing through the cabin.

To say I screamed was an understatement, my voice sounded like sharp nails being dragged along a chalk board, the pain had caused me to double over a dry heave due to the lack of food my stomach held.

During my desperate cries for help, his hands slowly raised up to his mask, grasping the ends of it as he slowly began to reveal himself. My breath hitched in my throat as I prepared myself, the entire time I had been here I had no idea what this man looked like. After all the beatings and punishments, I had no idea who was behind the mask.

I shut my eyes tightly, debating whether or not I wanted I wanted to see what this sick person looked like. I held my breath, my eyes squinted shut as I clung onto my broken arm extremely tightly.

I heard the soft sound of the mask falling to the floor but my eyes didn't open, I wanted to look but something was telling me not to.

I shook my head slightly, my bottom lip quivering as I sobbed slightly. "Open your eyes." He demand sternly.

I sucked in a small breath, the simply movement burned at my lungs. I pealed my eyes open slowly, allowing brain to process the person that was in front of me, the person that had beaten me senseless, the person that had starved me of real food, the person who ruined my life.

"B-beau...".

Chapter 20

Jai's POV

The familiar piercing green eyes that were once hidden behind the mask were now gazing evilly into my own. Though they weren't the kind eyes I had once known, instead they held a look of pure hatred. Though the familiar face staring at me hadn't brought comfort like it was supposed to, now I knew what he was capable of, I was terrified.

I didn't understand, my mind was buzzing like a puzzle in desperate need to be put together, nothing added up, my heart was aching with betrayal and confusion.

This entire time, all the beatings, the harsh words and neglect, this entire time my own flesh and blood was behind all of this. He was the reason my body ached painfully, he was the reason my stomach growled in hunger, he was the reason my body had literally given up itself. He was the reason I went missing. Yet I still didn't understand.

"W-why?" I whispered, my voice was full of hurt and betrayal. I wanted to cry, but due to the lack of water my body had become dehydrated.

Beau shook his head, an unpleasant smirk playing at his lips. I searched his features for some sign, a sign that the living brother I once knew was there, but nothing. Instead stood someone I didn't know.

He slowly crouched down to my level, his smirk remaining. His hand slowly reached towards my achingly broken arm, but I weakly shuffled away before he could lay a hand on me. Again.

"You always were the favourite, weren't you." He chuckled darkly, his eyes clouding over slightly.

I refused to believe that the boy crouching in front of me is my brother, this was not my brother. My brother was loving and caring, not this malicious monster. My bottom lip quivered slightly as I shook my head, avoiding his intimating gaze as much as I could.

"Always got what you wanted, mummy's little boy, you never did a single thing wrong in her eyes." He grinned evilly, his hand roughly grasping my jaw as he snapped my head to face him.

"Every single thing you did, you got away with." He fingers tightened around my chin harshly, causing me to hiss in pain.

I had no idea where he was going with this, I was still clueless. Mum had always treated the three of us equally, she always managed to buy us everything we needed. She always took good care of us. The three of us.

"Because of you, I was pushed aside." He growled, he grabbed my arm harshly as he tightly squeezed, causing me to yelp out in pain and fear. The pain shot through my arm like bolts of lightening, I knew for a fact that it was definitely broken.

"All those stupid awards you won, all your amazing grades." His eyes were dark but his grin was wide, showing all of his teeth.

My heart was breaking. I thought that all of my achievements would make my mother and brothers proud of me, I strived hard for them. We grew up on little money, I had put my heart and soul into doing well in school to help provide for me and my family, this wasn't supposed to happen. I didn't mean to push Beau aside, I didn't mean to hog all of the attention, I just wanted to help.

"I'm s-sorry." My voice came out as a low whisper, feeling mentally and physically weak.

I hoped Beau would see what he's doing to me, I hoped that something inside of him would just suddenly snap him back to how he was. This was so overwhelming, seeing my once loving and caring brother transform into a cruel monster right before me, yet I still had no real understanding of why my attempts of help would anger him.

"So weak." He chuckled, rolling his eyes as he released his grip on my arm. I was suddenly struck with a harsh force, my cheek instantly throbbing from the impact. My hand raised to my mouth, blood automatically pouring from the new wound. I coughed slightly as the taste of blood over took my senses.

"Mum favoured you Jai, mine and Luke's achievements were always over looked because of you!" His voice suddenly roared, anger was clearly evident. His eyes burned with hatred and he stared at me furiously.

My intentions were never to steal the attention from Luke or Beau, that's the last thing I'd ever do. I just wanted to make my family proud, but I didn't realise that my constant achievements would push Beau and Luke aside. I just wanted them to be proud of me.

"And for that, you will pay."

Before I could even question his motives his fist collided with my stomach fiercely, knocking the wind out of me as I gasped desperately for air. I choked on my sobs as I inhaled as much air as I could possibly could. My arms wrapped protectively around my stomach, hoping to prevent further hits.

His fists harshly grasped a lock of my hair, roughly pulling my head up to look him in the eye. The thing that terrified me most was that he showed no intention of stopping his violent act, he showed no regret.

"Beau! Please!" I coughed violently, blood instantly spluttering from my mouth as his foot repeatedly connecting with my stomach. He blocked out my pleas for help. I could feel my throat tightening, my head was becoming lighter and lighter by the second and little spots slowly began taking over my vision.

The kicks stopped, but I was far too weak and damaged to even consider moving. I felt Beau kneel down besides me, sweeping a piece of hair away from my face before leaning down to my ear. "No one will ever know." He whispered, I could sense his smirk.

I watched through squinted eyes has he exited the room as nothing happened and soon enough my steady breaths came to a halt as darkness engulfed me.

Chapter 21

L uke's POV

Four months later

To say I wasn't myself was an understatement, without Jai by my side I had become a completely different person. When he went missing, my happiness went missing too. I don't remember the last time I laughed or even smiled. A dark grey cloud hung over my head and followed me everywhere I went.

My nights had become sleepless, I tossed and turned until I became frustrated. I was lucky to get at least an hour of sleep each night, but even then I would be awoken by nightmares.

I still had hallucinations quite frequently, I'd see blood seeping from almost every inch of the house but I had grown used to my mind toying with me now.

I had a small calendar on my wall and each day I'd mark how many days Jai had been missing in hopes he'd return home the following day. But so many days had passed that I eventually gave up marking down the days.

I'd never been away from Jai for so long before, this was the longest I'd ever been without him and boy was I suffering. I missed him by my side, I missed his lame jokes and contagious laughter, I missed playing video games with him and our movie nights. I missed him.

Mum had eventually returned to work, last week was her first day back. I could see she had no motivation or energy to wake up at silly times in the morning, but she still forced herself to go as she wanted to provide for Beau and I.

Beau locked himself away in his room everyday, I hardly ever saw him. But when I did, he would simple glare at me before hiding away in his room again. I guessed he was still mad at me for what I did. I didn't mean for it to cause harm, I just wanted someone to see the same things I was seeing, even if they weren't real. I didn't want to feel crazy.

I hadn't returned to school yet, instead the teachers sent work to my house so I could still keep up with my education. I didn't even want to think about going to school any time soon, trying to focus on the work being sent to my house was hard enough. I was thankful that my teachers understood.

It was Saturday today which meant mum had the day off work, she wanted to stay home in her pajamas but she had forced herself to get up and go shopping since our cupboards were basically empty. I stayed home though, I hadn't left the house in ages and I didn't plan on leaving any time soon.

I flicked aimlessly through the channels on the television but nothing interesting caught my eyes, besides, my mind was way too occupied for me to even focus on watching television, I just wanted some background noise since Beau wasn't going to come out of his room any time soon.

I sighed, letting my arm fall onto the sofa as I flicked to a random channel. I was bored, but I'd never allow myself to have any fun when my brother was missing, I hadn't even see James or Daniel since the day it happened.

They'd tried texting me but I never responded. I had isolated myself from everyone except from mum and Beau.

I ran my hands over my face as I sighed softly, I had literally lost myself. I never knew what to do with myself anymore. I felt so alone without Jai. Everyday I would wait on wait for a phone call saying that Jai had been found and every night I prayed for that phone call. But no luck so far.

I heard Beau's door squeak open as he exited his room, his was wearing fresh clothes and his face held the same scowl he always shot me every time he saw me. He'd changed so much since Jai went missing, he'd become more angry and annoyed, especially towards me. I was still shocked that he had hit me the other day, he'd never laid a hand on me before. I still had a purplish bruise from the impact. But I forgave him, he's hurting just as much as I am.

I was pulled from my thoughts by my mum kicking open the front door as she struggled through with numerous bags of shopping. I instantly shot up from my seat to help mum with the shopping.

"Thanks sweetheart." She huffed breathlessly as I retrieved a few of the plastic carrier bags she struggled to hold. I just simply nodded in response.

"Go take those into the kitchen whilst I get the rest from the car." She ordered as she patted my back gently before returning back to the car.

The bags were heavy but I'd managed, I trudged them through the hallway and into the kitchen where I gently set them on the floor. Standing up straight as I huffed slightly, catching my breath, Beau's presence instantly caught my eye and when I had processed what he was doing, I felt anger boil in the pit of my stomach.

There he stood in front of the sink, a bowl of fake blood in his left hand whilst his right hand held a syringe. He hadn't seen me, so I continued to quietly observe his actions. He inserted the syringe into the bottom of the tap before squirting a fair amount of fake blood into it. His sudden movements caused me to hide behind the door frame where I could observe him without getting caught.

He quickly hid the bowl and fake blood under the sink.

"Oi Luke! Get your ass in here and do the dishes!" He demanded as he wiped his hands against his jeans.

The anger bubbled in the pit of my stomach as I soon came to realisation of what was happening. The hallucinations, they weren't real, Beau was behind them all. He knew that the second I turned on the tap to do the dishes, the taps would ooze with the fake blood that he purposely put there.

Thanks to him, I had gotten myself into trouble so he or mum wouldn't think I was crazy for seeing these things. Thanks to him, I'd been terrified to even step foot in a shower again, thanks to him I was tricked into believing that I was losing my mind.

What do you guys think?

Chapter 22

- -

Luke's POV.

My blood boiled immensely, burning as it soared through my veins. I wasn't going crazy, everything I saw was actually there, all thanks to Beau. I wanted to understand why he would would do this, but I just couldn't. He knew perfectly well the seriousness of the situation but he still continued to mess around. I knew he was a jokester, but I didn't expect him to take things this far.

"Why?" I questioned, hurt was evident in my voice.

His face held a smirk, a sickening smirk and I was beginning to feel uncomfortable under his gaze.

I looked at him in disbelief, my mouth hanging open slightly. I was beyond shocked, to think that Beau would even think that this was funny made my stomach churn, I was all for joking around but to pull something like that during our current situation was out of order.

"Why what, Luke?" He chuckled, his voice was low. He stepped away from the sink, slowly walking past me but not once did he break eye contact. He leant against the wall with his right foot against it whilst his arms crossed across his chest, his smirk still playing on his lips.

"You know what you're doing!" My anger soon enough over powered my sadness as I screamed in sudden rage. My emotions were all over the place, but that was nothing new, but what Beau had done just added fuel to the fire.

"Do I?" He grinned teasingly, his eyes were no longer their usual bright green. Instead they were a dull moss green that didn't look so friendly anymore.

My hands balled into tight fists by my side, my knuckles turning white. I was trying with everything in me to hold myself from lashes out on him, but his stupid smirk made it extremely difficult.

"I'm not crazy, it was all you!" My jaw clenched tightly as my hands shook slightly, I could feel the anger slowly soaring through my body with every passing second.

He pushed himself up from the wall as he began walking slow circles around me, his eyes boring into my own. His lips were pulled into a giant sly smile, everyone of his teeth on display. His behaviour was honestly scaring me, this wasn't my big brother.

"Are you sure about that?" He chuckled, inching closer to me slowly.

My breathing hitched in slight fear but I remained strong. I responded with a simple nod, keeping my face as straight as I possible could. I wouldn't let him know he was getting to me, he'd enjoy it too much.

"How'd you know you weren't just hallucinating what just happened?" He grinned teasingly. I knew exactly what he was trying to do, he was trying to get inside my head, trying to continue making me believe I was crazy but I know what I saw. And I wouldn't allow him to mess with me.

My body shook as the anger bubbled, I gritted my teeth together tightly and before I knew it, my left arm was pulled back before roughly connecting with Beau's nose. His hands instantly shot up to his now blood nose as he tumbled back slightly. I couldn't control myself, I pushed his shoulders harshly, sending him falling to the floor.

"I AM NOT CRAZY!" My lungs burned from how loud I screamed.

I was shocked, and I could tell by the look on Beau's face that he was too. But his facial expressions were soon replaced by anger. His eyes grew darker as he pushed himself up from the kitchen floor, standing right in my face intimidatingly.

"You're not crazy huh?" He smirked tauntingly, wiping away the blood that had trickled from his nose onto his upper lip.

In the corner of his eyes I could see his arm pulled back, ready to connect with my stomach but before he even had the chance to hit me, I harshly grabbed his wrist in prevention.

"What's going on in here?" Mums soft voice suddenly filled the air, the shopping bag rustled as she set them down on the floor. Thank god she's here. Beau's lips pulled into a devious smirk as he sucked in a deep breath. "Ah! My wrist! Let go!" He cried falsely.

"Luke! What are you doing!" Mum screeched. I felt her hands placed on my shoulders as she pulled me away from Beau, a look of disappointment drowning her features. I glanced behind her to see Beau with his usual smirk.

"What? No! He went to hit me!" I desperately cried in hopes she'd believe me, though I knew it was useless. Beau had always been the golden boy and I had always been the 'trouble maker'. It was obvious she was going to believe Beau.

"I didn't mum, he's been hallucinating again." He sighed dramatically, his fake act of sadness wrapping mum around his pinky finger.

"I'm not! It's been Beau this whole time! He even hid the fake blood under the sink!" I cried in utter desperation, I wasn't the bad guy here, not this time.

I harshly yanked the sink door open, hoping to reveal the blood and syringe Beau had hidden under there, but to my surprise it had gone, the only things in sight were dish clothes and washing up liquid. My eyes grew wide, they should be under there! That's where he had hidden them to!

"Luke, there's nothing there." Mum sighed, a hint of annoyance in her voice. She rubbed her hands over face tiredly, I knew she had a lot on her plate but I was not about to let Beau make me look like the bad guy.

"Mum I swear, please believe me..." I whispered, tears brimming my eyes before cascading down my cheeks. In the corner of my eyes I could see Beau with a very amused expression plastered across his face.

"Luke sweetheart, I think we should take you to see a therapist, this isn't normal." She spoke softly, her hand rubbing gentle circles on my back. My eyes were wide and my mouth hung open, I was honestly lost for words and nothing I could do or say would in anyway help in my defence.

Chapter 23

B eau's POV

I grinned in satisfaction as my little plan came to success, pretty good considering I thought it up on the spot. Not bad.

I knew mum wouldn't believe a word Luke said, after all he was the troubled child in the family. I however had always been the good one, always tried my best and always told the truth. Unlike Luke who managed to get himself in petty fights almost every day during school. Of course she wasn't going to believe him, I'd do everything in my power to make sure my plan is a success.

As for Jai, I was angry with him. I'm just doing what he deserves, he stole the attention from me, he stole the spotlight from me. Anything I could do he would do ten times better than me. It was that way ever since we were little, and now he's going to feel the pain and neglect that I had felt every time my achievements were dismissed because he had done it better.

What I was doing made sense to me, I was neglected, pushed aside and forgotten. So now it's his turn to feel neglected, pushed aside and forgotten.

The night we visited the asylum, I knew that it was the perfect time to hatch my plan. In the darkness where no one could see what was happening, how I pulled it off will remain a secret for now. Did I feel guilty? Not really. I was finally going to get my time to shine now that Jai's out of the picture.

Mum will miss him of course, but she'll get over it soon enough. I mean Luke's an exact replica of him, it's like he never went missing. Plus I'll make sure to make her proud, I'll make her forget about him sooner or later.

She's slowly getting back into her regular daily routine which is good, I'm sure it won't take long until we can return back to being a happy family.

I'll do what it takes to become mums favourite child.

Short chapter! Just wanted to give you a little look into Beau's thoughts!

Chapter 24

Luke's POV

I had little to no clue as to why Beau was acting the way he was. He'd always been such a sweet and caring big brother, he always looked out for Jai and I making sure that we were okay. He'd fight away all the bullies, he'd never let anyone lay a hand on us. To see him suddenly change from his old self to this broke my heart. My twin brother was missing and now I'm losing my big brother.

I was slowly growing scared of Beau, he'd send me dirty looks or his usual smirk every time he saw me, he'd managed to convince mum that I was the bad guy. I was scared he'd hit me again, I didn't want to be afraid of him.

Though I was still extremely angry towards me, I wouldn't dare let him see my fear. He'd feed from it and use it to weaken me, he's already turned my own mother against me. She thinks I've lost my mind, that the impact of losing Jai had sent me out of my mind. She thinks I'm violent towards Beau as well, when in reality it's all the opposite.

Beau had pretty much locked himself away in his room these last few days, it had been a week since the little incident in the kitchen. Which had also meant it had been another week had gone by without Jai. I'd lost count of how long he's been missing, it's been months and the pain hadn't gotten easier.

I sunk further into the sofa, allowing my thoughts to drown me. This was usual for me now. I'd lost interest in almost every thing, I'd lost contact with James and Daniel. Whether Beau had been to see them I didn't know, but I really couldn't care.

"I've booked you a session with a therapist." Mums voice pulled me from my thoughts.

She walked into the living room before taking a seat besides me, her pink robe wrapped around her whilst her hands cupped her mug of hot tea.

"I don't need to see a therapist." I rolled my eyes.

It was true, I didn't need to see a therapist. Talking about my feelings to some stranger wouldn't make things better for me, unless this therapist can wave a magic wand a bring Jai back to me, then it was useless and a waste of money. Besides, if anything Beau was the one who needed a therapist here, not me.

"Living in denial is going to make things worse." Mum sipped at her tea, glancing at me every now and then.

It frustrated me, I wish she'd believe me for once. But unless I had caught Beau in his little act and somehow managed to provide evidence then that would be seemingly impossible.

I decided to ignore her, I knew she wouldn't believe me so there was no point in arguing. She'd have to drag me out of this house kicking and screaming to even get me anywhere near this therapist, it just wasn't going to happen.

"Why won't you let me help you?" She sighed, placing her mug down on the wooden table besides her chair. She had a look of sadness which irritated me.

"You can start helping me by actually listening to me." I muttered, avoiding eye contact with her as I gazed at the television screen.

"You're talking nonsense Luke." She shook her head in disappointment.

I chose to ignored any further comments she made, it would just end up with me losing my temper if I fought back, which would just add to mums theory of me 'losing my mind'.

The living room quickly fell into an awkward silence, the television on low in the background. I wasn't actually watching whatever was on, I just hoped mum would think I was so she'd stop with the talking. I didn't want to talk if my words meant nothing.

We sat in silence for a few minutes, I could tell mum was dying to speak up and say something but I made sure I'd look interested in whatever was happening on the television, even though couldn't care less.

I jumped slightly at the sound of a car door slamming, I glanced out of the window to see Beau seated in the passenger seat in his car. Where was he going? Thoughts flooded my mind, maybe he's going out to buy more things that'll somehow make me look like the bad guy, this could be my chance to catch him out.

"Um, I'm gonna go lay down." I mumbled, pushing myself up from the seat. Mum simply nodded without a word, I knew she was pissed at me but I had bigger things to worry about. Like whatever Beau was up to.

I eagerly walked through the hallway before entering my bedroom, slamming the door shut behind me. I stumbled and shoved everything that was on my floor out of the way, if Jai was here with me now he'd kill me, he hated when I left my things all over the bedroom floor.

I forced the window up, carefully swinging both of my legs over the ledge. It was quite a jump to the floor but nothing too serious.

I huffed in a breath before heaving myself off of the ledge, landing on the floor with a hard thump. "Shit." I muttered as I quickly brushed myself off.

I spotted mine and Jai's bikes leant up against the wooden fence, they were quite old but it'll do. I fought of the thoughts of when Jai and I used to ride our bikes along the streets pretending we were professional racers. I needed to focus.

I could see Beau's car pull out of the drive way before taking on the road, I took no time to hop on the bike and begin peddling. I needed to keep a reasonable distance between Beau's car and myself so he wouldn't see me, it's not like I could trail behind him on an old bike anyway.

I had made sure to keep my phone in my pocket on camera mode ready, I was going to catch him out and prove to mum that this entire time it was Beau behind my 'hallucinations'. I didn't know where he was going but I silently hoped that it would be something worth following him for. Mum needed to know what he was doing, this was hopefully my chance to prove myself.

The wind brushed through my curly locks, grazing at my cheeks which resulted in my cheeks and nose turning a rosy red colour.

The weather was glum but dry thankfully, the gravel crackling underneath the bikes tyres as I put all my energy at peddling. My heart beat was beginning to quicken but I'd work through it.

Beau's car was quite a distance away but I could still keep a good view on it. All of my surroundings began blurring and fuzzy as I sped past them, my main focus was on Beau's car. It was like everything was bluffing except for his car.

I felt guilty for wanting to catch him out, I mean he had always been an amazing brother to me until now. I never would've thought that Beau even had this side to him and I honestly didn't want to know. My heart ached for the old caring Beau to comfort me, not the Beau that suddenly manipulated mum into thinking I was crazy.

Tears brimmed my eyes but were quickly dried by the constant gusts of wind brushing past my face.

I watched carefully as Beau made a sharp left turn, pulling into what seemed to be a forest trail. I furrowed my eyes as I tightened my hands around the brakes, hiding behind a bush as I watched him. He had parked his car before exiting it, he had set off on the trail by foot.

What the hell was he doing out here? Maybe he came out here to think? Something told me to follow him anyway.

I dumped my bike to the side, I wasn't even worried if someone would take it since it was outdated anyway.

I mentally cursed as little twigs and rocks crumbled and cracked underneath my feet, I needed to be as quiet as possible but it was proving difficult.

The trees stood extremely tall, their leaves had created a slight roof over the forest, it honestly did look beautiful. There were various birds nests resting on every other branches were little baby birds were sleeping in some.

I trailed behind Beau, making sure to stay hidden as much as I possibly could. The only reason I could think of him driving out here was so he could sit down and think, to be honest I didn't even know this forest existed, even though I'd spent my entire life living in AUS.

I heard a faint whistle come from Beau, I watched as his hands dug deep into his pocket before he pulled out a single cigarette and lighter, lightening the tip of the cigarette before placing it between his lips.

He seemed to know the path he was walking on very well, he seemed confident in where he was going. Though we'd never visited this place before.

I could see what seemed to be an old wooden cabin in the distance, the thing looked like it would just fall apart any second. The positioning of it looked extremely uneven, the wood looked damp and groggy.

Confusion washed over me as Beau pulled out a small key before jogging up to the front of the cabin, he pushed the key into the door before opening it. How on earth does he even have a key for this thing? Maybe he's watching it for a friend? But the cabin looked so old, why would any of his friends even consider owning it?

I was pulled out of my little trail of confused thoughts by a screech of terror echoing through the forest. My eyes widened and my heart rate sped up as I slowly creeped towards the cabin.

"Don't hurt me!" The voice pleaded.

I knew in a heart beat who's voice it was.

Chapter 25

Luke's POV

"Jai..." I whispered, my heart instantly shattered into numerous of pieces. I didn't know whether to feel relieved by the sound of his voice or terrified by the fear in his voice. Months without him by my side, without his smile or his laugh, he was just a few centimetres from me.

The person I had be longing for this entire time, to hear his voice again and to see him smile again, he was in there.

"Stop!" His voice screeched, pain laced within. My breath hitched and everything felt numb, he was hurt. He was hurting, I needed to get to him fast. But my mind was still having trouble processing the fact that after all these months I'll finally see his face again.

I pressed my ear against the wooden cabin, hoping to get a better hearing on what was happening. My heart thumped heavily against my chest as various emotions ran through my body.

"Can I help you?" A familiar voice chuckled, instantly making me snap my head into the direction of the voice.

Relief washed over me as I noticed James stood behind me, I'm positive he'll help me get to Jai.

"J-James oh thank god!" I cried, my emotions were getting the best of me as my eyes brimmed with tears, I just couldn't wait to have Jai back home with me again where no one will hurt him, I'd make sure of that.

"C-come on! You h-have to help me get Jai out of t-there!" I stumbled over my words as a rush of adrenaline powered through my veins. Part of me wanted to bust this cabin down and run to Jai's rescue but another part of me was terrified of what I would be facing.

"I don't think so." James chuckled, shaking his head. There was a dark look hidden beneath his eyes which made my insides twist. The same dark look that Beau's eyes held.

"W-hat do you mean?" I questioned.

"Beau's paying me to help him, I need the money bro." James grinned a sickening grin.

My insides churned with anger, my own brother and best friend. How could they? Why would they! Why would Beau even considering hurting his own flesh and blood! After everything we've through together as a family, after all the promises we made as brothers, all the memories we created! How could he!

"You make me sick." I spat angrily. I had no idea who James and Beau were anymore.

My heart hurt, after all these months of worry and grieving over Jai, sleepless nights wondering if he was even alive, Beau knew this entire time. He saw how much I was hurting, he heard my cries and saw my tears, yet he remained silent about the situation the entire time.

Adrenaline pumped eagerly through my veins, I clenched my fists and gritted my teeth angrily before gathering up all of my energy before heaving it against the wooden door.

The door fell to the floor, landing with a loud thump which had caused dust particles to swarm the dark room. The little bit of sunlight shon through the gaping hole, lightening up the scenery.

"J-Jai o-oh my god Jai." My heart had jumped into my throat, my body feeling numb as tears effortlessly streamed my cheeks.

There he was, my baby brother, after all these months.

He sat in the far left corner shaking, he looked so much more thinner, his bones poked through almost every inch of his skin, dark bags hung under his dull eyes as well. His hair was a matted mess on top of his head, he looked dead. If it weren't for the terrified eyes boring back into my own I would've thought he was dead.

I took no time to race to his aid, gently pulling him into my comforting embrace. He didn't say a word, I could only make out the small shaky breaths that shook his body. I wanted to squeeze him, never let him out of my sight again but I didn't want to hurt him, he was so fragile.

"I'm sorry, i'm so sorry." I violently sobbed, shakily running my hands through his matted hair. He remained silent, he didn't even make an effort to move. By the sight of him I knew he was very weak and ill. He didn't even look like my Jai.

I felt a strong sense of relief to have him near me again, I had missed him so much and words can't even describe the amount of worry I was left with.

"C-come on, I'm going to get you out of here." I gently cupped his face with my hands, my voice weak and shaky due to the overpowering emotions searing through me.

I carefully removed him from my embrace, observing his injuries. His body was covered with colourful bruises, both of his knees were severely grazed and his left arm looked extremely out of place. "Oh god." I whimpered as I gently took his left arm in my hands, the broken bone was almost piercing his skin.

The clothes he wore were extremely tatty and torn, they couldn't even be classed as clothes anymore. Carefully, I removed the groggy white 'shirt' from his body before tossing it carelessly. I removed my warm baggy jumper before helping Jai into it. It broke my heart to see how loose it know looked on him, he'd lost so much weight of was terrifying.

"C-Come on." I shakily whispered. I had no idea how I was going to get him back home, he could barley keep his head up, let alone stand on two feet. I gently hooked my arms underneath his armpits, steadily lifting him as slow as I could without hurting him. He whimpered softly as his legs began shaking slightly. "I'm sorry." I whispered, tears trickling along my cheeks knowing the amount of pain he was in.

I didn't know what to do, my phone had no signal since we were located quite deep into the forest. And Jai didn't have the strength of energy to walk to a main road, even with my assistance. I had to somehow carry him to a main road and wave someone down to help. I nodded in agreement with myself as I managed put together my little escape plan.

"And where do you think you two are going?" A familiar voice boomed.

Chapter 26

Luke's POV

I grimaced at the sound of his voice before meeting his familiar green eyes. They showed no sorrow or regret. His youngest brother was laying pretty much lifeless in my arms all because of him, yet not even the slightest hint of sorrow showed. I'd become terrified around Beau, his presence sent chills along my spine and knowing that this was all his idea made my head spin.

But my current anger and hatred from his had subsided for the time being, my mind set was fixed on getting Jai help as soon as possible, but as soon as I could get my hands on Beau then I know what I'd do.

"C-come on Beau! He's going to die!" I eagerly pleaded glancing down at Jai. He was limp in my arms, his chest was barley moving and his eyes were glued shut. If it were for the tiny pulse that thumped against his neck then I honestly would've thought he was dead.

I gently placed my two fingers against his neck again, feeling the tiny rhythm of his weak pulse fluttering. Every time I checked for a pulse it seemed to get weaker and weaker and I was terrified that at some point his pulse won't be there when I check.

Beau shook his head, and evil grin crept upon his lips as he spoke. "That's a shame." He chuckled, taking a few steps closer.

I couldn't acknowledge his words, I just needed to get Jai out of here. In this exact moment, I wasn't scared of Beau, I was scared of his words or what he would do. I was scared of losing Jai. Again.

Jai stirred slightly, he was far too weak and I was absolutely terrified that he would just give up any minute now.

"B-beau please! P-please don't let him die." I sobbed violently, pulling Jai as close to me as possible could, afraid that he would just slip away from me. I was becoming frustrated and Beau certainly wasn't helping.

"Beau for gods sake please! Please let me help him! Please!" I suddenly screeched as I became overwhelmed and frustrated with the situation.

"Hmm, maybe in a few hours." He sighed dramatically with his usual signature grin playing on his lips. He knew very well that Jai wouldn't be able to hold an for another hour.

I gritted my teeth as tears effortlessly fell from my eyes, landing onto Jai's face. "Come on Jai, please keep fighting, you can't leave me again." I shakily whispered in his damp matted hair, hoping that my words would help to at least some extent.

I gulped slightly before once again pressing my fingers gently against his neck, his pulse had decreased again, it was still there but very lightly. My heart beat increased as I knew Jai was slowly slipping away from me. I wanted to throw up from the fear of losing him again, I couldn't lose him again.

I could see Beau's facial features alter slightly, a glimpse of concern flashes across his face but his evil grin remained.

"Beau...come on please...you can't let him die." I sobbed into Jai's hair, rocking him slowly and gently.

Beau took a few steady steps towards me before crouching down in front of me. He harshly grabbed my face with one hand, his fingers digging into my cheeks as he snapped my neck to face him. "You better keep your damn mouth shut, you understand me?" He sneered, his eyes clouding over as glanced between Jai and I.

He grabbed a fistful of my hair, pain shooting through my scalp as he did so. He grinned a toothy grin before pulling an object out from his back pocket. He held the object up in front of my eyes, allowing me to analyse what it was. A pocket knife. It had already been stained with blood, Jai's blood.

My eyes widened at the sight of the knife before I eagerly pulled Jai closer to me. "Do not hurt him." I hissed.

"This isn't for him." He chuckled.

Before I had the chance to respond a searing pain shot through my scalp, blood instantly began trickling along my cheek. I didn't react, I was more thankful that he hadn't hurt Jai again.

He held up a few strands of my hair with a sickening smile, before throwing the few strands around the room. An accomplished smile proud on his face.

"Now we can go."

Without any words I held Jai tight in my embrace, heaving myself up from the floor with a huff. He wasn't even at all, in fact he was sickeningly light which made my stomach churn with anger. This was all Beau's fault.

"Not you." He chuckled at me as he rolled his eyes.

"I'm going with him!" I angrily shouted. If Beau thinks I'm leaving Jai on his own with him again then he's got another thing coming. I will not allow him to hurt him again, not over my dead body.

"No you're not." He sang with his stupid grin.

"James!" He shouted, his voice bouncing off of the wooden walls.

On que, James entered the room with a look of sorrow. I know Beau had forced him into this situation but I was still extremely mad at as well. My best friend and my brother, I just couldn't understand. Beau nodded at James sending him some kind of signal which James immediately reacted to.

"I'm sorry." James mouthed before his fist collided harshly with my ribs, the pain shot through my body unbearably, I instantly dropped Jai onto the wooden flooring as I gasped for air. The punch had knocked the wind out me.

"Now." I heard Beau's voice demand strictly.

The sound of rustling filled my ears as a plastic bad was held over my head, my arms suddenly bound behind my back as my body was lifted. "No! Please! Jai! Help Jai!" I cried as I thrashed around but their grip was extremely strong. I felt myself being carried away outside as the sun beamed down on my exposed skin.

"It's too late to help him." A sickening voice whispered in my ear with a snicker.

Chapter 27

Beau's POV

The car engine came to life with a stutter. I had ordered James to sit in the back seat of the car to keep Luke under control as I knew he'd do everything he could to get back to Jai. I knew what I was doing was extremely wrong and incredibly illegal, I was leaving my baby brother to die but for some reason my mind was more focused on keeping myself out of trouble rather than helping him.

The broken branches and rocks snapped underneath the thick tires as I carelessly pulled out onto the main road. Trying to look as normal as possible, I didn't want to look suspicious.

I honestly didn't intend for things to go this far, my plan was only to get Jai out of the way for a while so I'd have more attention. My intentions weren't to hurt him but something inside of me snapped and the more he annoyed me, the angrier I became with him.

I would go to the ends or the earth to keep myself innocent, if mum knew the truth behind the situation then she'd completely disown me. Which is why I had already hatched a plan to prevent that from happening.

But the fact that Luke was aware of what was happening made things so much more harder, I knew he wouldn't keep his mouth shut and he'd just end up throwing me into the deep end and completely spill the truth to mum. But I wouldn't allow that to happen, I had messed with his head once and I wasn't afraid to do it again.

My thoughts were pulled to a halt by Luke harshly kicking the back of my chair, his screams of anger filling the silence. I wanted to feel bad but I just couldn't.

"Control him, James." I spat, glancing at Luke in the mirror. His face was bright red, his eyes were full of hatred and anger. I had restrained his arms behind his back to make sure that he wouldn't get far if he were to escape.

"You're going to pay! I swear to god you're going to regret every little move you've made!" Luke hissed, his words laced with nothing but anger. Little veins popped up on his neck as he struggled to free himself from the tape that held his wrists together.

I simply rolled my eyes. His words meant nothing to me, just a bunch of empty threats.

"Sure I am." I chuckled teasingly, knowing very well that this would provoke him. He reacted with a harsh kick to the back of my seat, causing me to jolt forward slightly.

"Do that one more time and I promise you that you'll end up like Jai." I suddenly snapped, slamming my feet against the breaks as I twisted around in my seat to face him. I had roughly grabbed him by the strings of his hoodie which had completely taken him by sunrise as his eyes widened.

He looked completely lost for words, as did James. It made me feel powerful knowing that I had this slight control over them. Knowing I could scare them both like that made me feel strong and tall. Something I had never felt up until now. And boy did it feel good.

"You're a mental case." Luke snickered, I knew he was fighting the urge to kick the back of my seat again just by the way his legs bounced frantically up and down.

Throughout the car ride James had remained silent. I didn't want to drag him into to this but he was honestly a great help due to his strength. I had promised him a thousand dollars if he were to help me, but you and I both know I won't be paying him. I don't even have that kind of money, I'm shocked James actually fell for it but I'm not complaining.

I glanced at the two in the back seat before making a sudden turn off of the main road, pulling into a quiet alleyway not too far from our house.

"Alright, you will keep your mouth shut. Do not mention a single to thing to mum, do you understand me?" I hissed, turning around in my seat to face Luke. A sly smirk began playing upon his lips.

"And if I don't?"

I scowled at him before digging into the little pocket located on my car door, the familiar item connected with my skin. I pulled out the pocket knife before flicking the blade up in front of Luke. His smirk soon turned into a look of fear. I gently presses the knife against his stomach, not adding any kind of pressure to it.

"Maybe next time I won't be too generous." I chuckled.

His eyes widened as he gulped the lump in his throat, he nodded his head not even daring to utter another word. I had him right where I wanted him.

"James, use this to release his arms before we get to the house." I ordered with a strict tone. I carelessly tossed the pocket knife into the back seat, earning a slight hiss from James as the blade nipped at his fingers. "Oops." I cackled.

"And Luke? Remember what I said, even think of telling mum or running then I'll make sure that the knife pierces your skin next time." I glared at him through the mirror, a look of terror settled upon his features as James gently cut the rope that held his hands together.

Chapter 28

T hird Persons POV.

"Beau please, just take me back to him! Let me help him! I swear I won't tell anyone!" Luke pleaded in desperation. The two had just dropped James off at his house and were now headed back home. Beau had selfishly lied to Luke, he wasn't going to help Jai. And as much as Luke pleaded and cried, he still wouldn't. No, it would ruin his plan that would take place that night.

"No." Beau replied, a hint of boredom in his voice. Luke had begged and pleaded for him to turn around, which he constantly replied with a blunt 'no'.

Luke held the urge to pound the back of Beau's seat harshly, but he had become afraid of what Beau was capable of and didn't want to risk getting hurt. It would only anger Beau more. "Beau...please!" Luke whimpered. The anger that was previously laced in his voice had drowned in sadness. His eyes stung with tears as his bottom lip quivered.

"He's fine." Beau replied bluntly, his eyes fixed on the quiet road in front of him.

He was calm, his voice didn't hold any emotion other than boredom and he just hoped Luke would give up on the begging soon.

"He's not fine! He can't even hold his head up on his own!" Luke cried, hoping that some sense would finally come to Beau. Tears streamed down his pale cheeks as the road led them both further and further away from their brother.

Beau gripped the steering wheel, his jaw clenching slightly. He began to ignore Luke, which only infuriated Luke even more.

The remaining two minutes of the car ride back home was full of Luke's desperate sobs and attempts of convincing Beau to turn around. Though none of them proved to be successful as Beau had remained silent the entire time, ignoring his brothers pleads.

"Alright, like I said. If you even utter a single word to mum I will make sure you will regret it. Got it?" Beau turned around in his seat to face Luke, his calm manner suddenly switching into an angered one. He needed to frighten Luke into keeping his mouth shut.

Luke nodded, tears escaping from his eyes as he gazed at Beau. It was safe to say that he was now terrified of him, but that wouldn't stop him from trying all he could to save his brother.

"Now wipe your tears, you look like a baby." Beau replied in annoyance as he unbuckled his seatbelt and exiting the car. Luke gently wiped over his face with the sleeve of his hoodie, but part of him hoped that mum would see his tears and sense that something was wrong.

The two boys entered the house, the television was playing quietly whilst the sound of sizzling directed them to the kitchen. They trumped into the kitchen to greet their mother who was standing over the oven in her favourite apron, cooking what seemed to be burgers. It surprised Luke to see his mother cooking, usually work had drained most of her energy that they just ended up ordering in.

"Hey mum!" Beau smiled happily, placing a kiss on her cheek as his false smile reached his eyes. Luke knew Beau was only putting on an act but it made him miss his brother he once knew. "Hey sweetheart." Mum smiled slightly, it was obvious she was completely drained and tired.

Luke quietly slipped into the seat, resting his head against the kitchen table to hide the tears that were threatening to fall. He had promised himself that he'd bring Jai home safely, but now he knew where he was and he couldn't even do anything about it. He felt like he had failed him. He felt that he should've stood up to Beau no matter what the consequences were, He should've been brave for him.

"You okay Luke?" Mum questioned, adjusting the heat on the oven before pulling out a chair next to him. He raised his head, noticing Beau had left the room. This was his chance, He didn't care what Beau would do to him, all he cared about is bringing Jai home safely, even if that meant him getting hurt.

"I-I know w-where Jai is..." He whispered, his breath shaking as a familiar lump formed in his throat. His hands shook violently but he hid them discretely under the table.

Mums eyes widened in slight hope, tears instantly brimming them as her mouth hung open in shock. He could practically hear her heart beating. "Where is he? Where is my baby." She whimpered, her hands cupping his face lightly as her eyes bored into his.

He sucked in a deep breath, mentally preparing himself. This was it, he was completely throwing Beau under the bus. A slight part of him felt guilty, he was his big brother who he once cared dearly for. But his new attitude had honestly disgusted him, but he was still his big brother and a small piece of him would still care for him. He just couldn't believe that his own brother would even consider hurting Jai like that.

"Beau's hurting him." He closed my eyes, his breath hitching in his throat as the words left his mouth. His heart pounded against his chest violently.

He felt her warm hands leave his face, the sound of her chair scraping against the kitchen floor filled the sudden silence. He opened his eyes to see his mother stood glaring down at him, an angered expression fixed on her face.

"Go to your room." She shook her head in disappointment. Her knuckles were turning white as she held the tea towel tightly in her grip, almost as if she were stopping herself from hitting something.

"W-what?" He asked in disbelief. Why didn't she believe him? She had to believe him! He was telling the truth! His heart ached for her to open her eyes and realise what was happening, but Beau had somehow managed to blind her. "Go to your room!" She screeched in anger, her face was extremely red and her eyes were full fury.

"Please believe me..." He whispered. He glanced up at her with hopeful eyes.

She shook her head before turning her back to him, returning back to the oven. The sizzling of the burgers filled the silence as she ignored his presence. "Mum please believe me, I swear I'm telling the truth!" He pleaded, his voice cracked in sadness as his words left his mouth.

He felt heartbroken, his own mother didn't believe him. She didn't even take a second to process his words before she classed him as a liar. In her eyes, Luke was troubled, all those fights he had gotten into had definitely not helped this situation. Luke had always tried to bend the truth as a child, he understood why his mum wouldn't believe him. But he wished she knew that he wouldn't dare joke about in a situation like this.

She continued to ignore him, he shook his head as tears effortlessly fell from his eyes.

"What do I have to do to make you be-" His words were cut off by a harsh banging on the front door, he jumped at the sound.

"POLICE! OPEN UP!" A deep voice boomed from outside.

Gina's eyes widened in fright as her and Luke races to the front door, Beau already beating them to it as he opened the door revealing two police officers stood with stern faces. Blue and red lights flashing brightly behind them.

The two officers stormed into the house, harshly grabbing Luke by his arms before pinning them uncomfortably behind his back. "W-what's going on? Let go of me!" Luke cried as he felt something tight and cold connect with his wrists. Handcuffs.

"Luke Brooks you are under arrest for the murder of Jai Brooks." The police officer stated with a strict voice.

"What? He's not dead! I saw him! Please! He's still alive!" Luke cried out, his heart shattering into tiny pieces as the scene unfolded. Gina stood back, her hands shakily covering her mouth as she sobbed into them, Beau with a comforting arm around her.

"Our police department received an anonymous phone call directing us to Jai's location. Jai's body was discovered with numerous of lacerations and breaks. Luke Brooks' DNA was discovered at the scene. The case has now been upgraded from missing persons to murder. Anything you say or do will be held against you in court."

Chapter 29

- -

Luke's POV

I felt numb. All of the emotions that once swarmed my body had vanished and transformed into nothing. I felt empty. I felt like a shell of my former self. I sob my heart out in the back of the police car, but my cries were once again ignored. I wasn't crying for them to listen to me this time though. I was crying because he was gone. I'd never ever see his smile again or hear his laugh again. I'd never be able to create memories with him again.

It make me feel physically sick that the last memory I had of him was one I didn't want to remember. His helpless face will forever haunt me. How he didn't even have enough energy to speak. That's the last memory I will ever have of him.

I should've been brave for him. I should've gone back after him despite Beau's constant threats. Whatever Beau would've done to me would've hurt me a lot less than losing Jai. I'd should've endured the threats and helped Jai. But I wasn't as brave as he was, I'll never be as brave as he was. It shouldn't of been him, it should've been me.

Even though I was the one always getting into trouble and fights, putting up a tough a brave front, Jai was always the braver one than I was. He always saw the good in me when mum and Beau didn't. No matter how many fights I had gotten into, he always stood by my side. When I had gotten into trouble with the police before, he would never get angry at me. I could tell that he was disappointed, but never angry.

The things I'd do to bring him back. It seemed so surreal. Just a few hours ago he was alive, I held him as he struggled but he was still alive. He was still breathing and his heart was still beating. But a few hours later and his breaths came to a halt and his heart eventually stopped. Nothing pained me more than the fact that he was alone and scared when he died.

No matter how much I screamed at the sky and pounded my fists on the nearest item, no matter how many prayers I would say, I knew deep down it wouldn't bring him back. My mind was in a state of delusion. I had spent my entire life with him by myself but now I'd have to go on with the rest of my life without him.

I couldn't bare the thought of living without him, I wanted to be with him. If he couldn't be here with me then I wanted to be with him wherever he was. I desperately hoped that wherever he had gone he was happy and pain free, the only light in the situation was that he was no longer hurting. But that didn't make me feel any better, I just needed him back with me where he belonged. He didn't deserve this.

My thoughts were pulled to a halt by the sound of a door squeaking. I had been placed into a small room where I would be questioned by a detective. The room was small and extremely cold. A small metal table centred in the middle the room. Straight ahead of me was a huge mirror, but I had seen movies, I knew that there were people stood on the other side watching me with hatred. If only they would take the time to listen to the truth.

"Mr Brooks." A tall man who wore a smart black suit entered the room before taking a seat opposite me. His face was blank and held no emotion whatsoever.

"Please remind me of your relation to Jai Brooks." He ordered, pulling out a small black note book and a pencil before placing them in front of himself.

"I was his brother." I mumbled. My voice was pretty much dry from the amount of crying I had done, but I honestly didn't care how I looked or sounded right now.

He simply nodded before dotting a sentence together in his notebook before turning his attention back to me. "And you loved him, correct?" He question, his eyebrow raising slightly with his question. I instantly nodded, of course I loved him. We had our fights and arguments but throughout all of those I always loved him.

"Then why did you kill him?" The man with no name suddenly hissed, catching me off guard. I knew his tactic was to scare me into telling the truth, but the words that left my mouth were the complete truth.

"I didn't kill him." I whispered, shaking my head as tears brimmed my eyes again.

"The evidence proves differently." He muttered before once again jotting something down in his notebook. It was clear that he didn't care about my side of the story, Beau had managed to make me look like the bad guy and until I had a solid piece of evidence to prove my innocence then my story wouldn't be believed.

"The evidence our detectives discovered just so happen to contain your DNA. Not only were your finger prints found on Jai but a lock of your hair was also located at the scene." The man stated with a matter of fact tone.

I sniffled softly as I gazed down at the metal table, my heart just aching for everything to return to how it was. Aching for Jai to come back to me. I wanted this to be a nightmare that I would wake up from. I wanted to wake up to Jai annoyingly screeching in my ears.

"I held him yesterday, Beau had beaten him and I w-was trying to get him h-help." I stuttered over my words, the memories replaying in my head. Little did I know that would be the last time I'd ever see him again. I gulped slightly as the familiar lump formed in my throat, I wanted to just break down and sob my heart out. But I kept myself together. For Jai.

"I followed Beau a-and I heard Jai s-scream, that was the first time I had seen h-him since he went m-missing." It was a struggle for me to string a sentence together.

The man nodded before once again scribbling down on his notebook, I had no idea what he was writing but frankly I couldn't care. I fiddled with my hands slightly, the metal handcuffs that restrained my wrists were becoming slightly painful as they dug into my skin.

"You do realise that the evidence we have points to you? There's no trace of Beau Brooks' DNA at the scene. Can you explain that?" He questioned, his dull eyes boring into mine as he awaited my answer.

Truth was, I honestly couldn't explain that. I didn't know how Beau had managed to manipulate something like that but he did, he knew I wouldn't be able to explain it. I just simply shook my head whilst staring at my hands, droplets of tears landing onto the metal table. "I swear on my life that I didn't kill him." I cried.

My heart was beating rapidly against my chest as I struggled for breath through my frantic sobs. I couldn't take this, I couldn't take losing my brother, I couldn't take being pinned as the murder and I couldn't take my own family not believing me. I couldn't take any of it.

Chapter 30

Luke's POV

"Due to the lack of proof to prove your innocence you will not be allowed to leave the building until you're proven innocent during your court date. Until then you will held in a cell." The detective announced like it was nothing. Well to him it was nothing, he'd probably told thousands of people the same thing. But to me it was every thing.

Being accused and treated like a criminal until I'm proven innocent tore me to pieces, but the fact that I had to prove that I didn't murder my own brother shattered me even more.

I didn't know if I would mentally or physically be able to face all of this alone. All the difficult situations I had been faced with in life, Jai had always been by my side through them, helping me through them. But this time he wasn't and he will no longer be here to help me anymore.

"H-he can't be dead..." I whispered to no one but myself. I knew that I'd be living in denial for an extremely long time, I knew that I'd be waiting every single day for someone to tell me that it was all an mistake. Or it was all a dream.

"I'm sorry kid. The paramedics did their best but unfortunately his injuries were to severe. He most likely suffered a brain haemorrhage due to the amount of trauma to his head." The man uttered, not even looking me in the eye as the words left his mouth. But I wasn't convinced and I knew I never would be.

"A-are you sure? I-it might be a mistake!" I whimpered with a tiny glimpse of hope.

The man looked at me with dull eyes and sighed in annoyance. "When the paramedics arrived on the scene he was already gone. The EMT's did what they could but the damage was too severe, even if he had survived the trauma he would've been extremely brain damaged."

My heart beat began to increase at the new information. The amount of pain and suffering he had to endure. It explained why he couldn't move or talk when I held him those few hours ago. I brought my hands to my face, burying my face in them as I sobbed. Not caring how childish I sounded.

I was going kill Beau. He did this, this was his fault. He killed him, he hurt him and he hurt me. And he was going to pay.

"I'll be right back." The man stood up from his chair before exiting the room, locking the door with a click. There were two huge security guards stood outside the door as well, there was no way I was leaving this room with those two stood guard.

I couldn't control my tears, they kept falling and falling no matter how hard I tried to calm myself down. I couldn't face the fact that I'd never see Jai again, it was too much to take in. It overwhelmed me and literally destroyed me. We wouldn't have our movie night before bed again, I wouldn't be able to crack jokes with him again, he wouldn't be here to support me or see the good in me again. No, I was left alone with a family who thought of me as a monster. He left me and now I don't know what to do. He went to heaven and he left me in hell.

I honestly had no idea how I would manage without him, the thought of it pained me. I couldn't life in a world without him. I didn't want to. I wanted to be with him wherever he was. I'm positive my family wouldn't care if I left to be with him.

Short chapter but it's just a little filler chapter! The next one will be more interesting!

Chapter 31

Luke's POV

I could hear whispers bouncing around the room, though the voices were extremely muffled and I couldn't make out exactly what they were saying. The voices did sound extremely familiar though and brought me comfort.

Bolts of pain shot through my head every few seconds, the pain was so awful that it made my stomach churn. I wanted to reach up and hold my head but my limbs were frozen in place. Almost as if they were glued.

I began to panic. Why couldn't I move! Why can't I open my eyes! My heart rate began to speed up, I could feel it thumping against my chest as panic overcame me.

In the background, a rapid beeping sound overtook the whispers. I noticed the beeping sound was in sync with my heart beat. I heard people shuffling around, voices shouting at each other with what sounded like worry. I still couldn't understand what they were saying though.

I could feel people touching me, some were gentle whilst others were rough. I didn't know what they were doing though, but they seemed to be rushing. I wanted to shake them off of me! But I still couldn't move! I could hear them uttering commands and orders to each other. I didn't understand what was going on.

I couldn't see anything, every thing was dark. Though I was aware and alert but I was trapped in this darkness. I could feel people and hear people. I just couldn't see them or move my body.

I felt a sharp pain in the centre of my arm followed by a harsh burning sensation that travelled around my body instantly. I wanted to scream from the pain, but I could find my voice. The burning sensation travelled to almost every inch of my body before my muscles began to fall into a state of relaxation. My heart rate began to slow down regaining a steady pace and the same annoying beeping noise echoing in the background began to slow down in sync with my heart beat.

The voices relaxed and spoke in a much calmer manner, I felt a warm hand run through my hair softly. "Good job buddy." An unfamiliar voice whispered directly into my ear. I didn't recognise the voice at all. The hand left my hair and I assumed the person left the room judging by the sound of a door opening and closing.

I tried to best to understand what was happening but my brain just couldn't piece it together at all. I didn't understand where I was or who these people were. I didn't understand why I couldn't move or speak.

I felt a gentle embrace clutch my hand tightly, I wanted to pull away as there seemed to be something stuck in the back of my hand which dug into my skin when the person gripped my hand. It was uncomfortable but I couldn't pull away.

My thoughts wandered to my family. Where were they? Did they still love me? The only memory my brain had stored was being questioned in the police station about Jai's death. What happened after that was all a blur.

"Luke? Can you hear me?" A voice mumbled into my ear, it had a slight echo to it. The voice seemed sad, as if the person had been crying.

'Yes!' I thought. I wanted to scream that I could hear the person but no vocals left my mouth no matter how hard to forced it. The person sniffled quietly, they seemed like they were sobbing. They kept whispering sweet nothings into my ear and with each word the voice became clearer. I took it as a good sign, maybe my senses were slowly regaining their strength.

"I believe in you, Luke. You're tough kiddo, you can pull through this." The voice whispered into my ear. I could feel the persons grip loosen on my hand before a stroking sensation raised bumps along my arm.

What am I going to pull through? I thought to myself.

I could hear a door open with a click, the person who kept whispering me greeted whoever had entered. "I'm just going to take his vitals." The new voice was unrecognisable but sounded sweet and friendly. I didn't understand what 'vitals' were or why the person would be 'taking them'. But I hoped it wouldn't hurt.

The person stroking my arm moved away, I could hear their footsteps back away slightly. I instantly missed their touch, it was comforting and I suddenly longed for it again.

I felt someone place something cold into my left ear, followed by a high pitched beeping noise. "His temperature is perfect." The voice announced before the cold object was removed. The sound of Velcro sent shivers up my spine before something was wrapped firmly around my upper arm, with a beep of a button the object started to tighten around my arm slowly. I instantly wanted to rip whatever it was off of my arm, but again, still no movement.

"His blood pressure is a little high, but that's nothing concerning." The same voice spoke. The tight object was removed from my arm, an instant relief ran through my arm.

"I'm just going to check your heart and I'll leave you alone." The sweet voice spoke, running a soothing hand through my curls. I wondered if the person knew I could hear them, I mean they were talking to me as if I could.

Something extremely cold was placed against my chest which instantly made me jump slightly. "O-oh my god, d-did his hand j-just move?" A familiar voice interrupted in the back ground. "I think he did! Let's check!" The sweet voice announced with happiness, I could hear shuffling around but was suddenly distracted by something sharp being swiped up the bottom of my foot. My body instantly reacted as my leg jerked backwards.

"He's reacting to different sensations, I'm just going page his doctor."

My limbs tingled and tickled as they felt as if they were becoming lighter by the second, it was slowly becoming easier to move them, I couldn't move them a lot but they were slowly cooperating! I wasn't going to give up.

"Come on bud, squeeze my hand." The familiar voice encouraged before taking my hand lightly in their own. I gathered up all the energy my body had stored just to simple squeeze their hand and judging by their excited reaction, it had worked.

"He squeezed my hand! Oh my god!" The voice yelled happily, the echo from their voice sent pain through my head though I managed to push it aside.

"Excuse me, please." A deep voice ordered. I heard several people chattering excitedly in the background. Someone gently lifted my eyelid before shining an extremely bright light directly into my eyes. I couldn't see the person but I could see the light, it was almost blinding. "His pupils are reacting as well."

"Come on bud, you just gotta open your eyes!"

"You can do it, you've got this."

The several people in the room constantly mumbled encouraging words as they waited patiently. I needed to open my eyes. I needed to open my eyes. I needed to open my eyes. I kept repeating it over and over to myself as I slowly gathered the remaining energy my body had stored, I still felt extremely weak but I felt strong enough to open my eyes. I tried and tried to pry my eyes open and with each second the light became brighter and brighter.

Everything was extremely blurry, I could just about make out the different colours surrounding me. "My baby! You did it! Oh my baby!" A sweet voice cried as the person hovered over me. I could tell the person was female but I couldn't make out her features accurately yet. I could just tell that she had brunette hair.

I kept my gaze on her as my vision began to slowly focus on her features and within a few minutes I was instantly able to recognise her as my mother. "M-mum?" My voice was very weak, shaky and croaky and my throat burnt as the words left my mouth.

Her hazel eyes filled with tears as a smile spread across her lips, she nodded as the tears trickled along her cheeks, running her hand through my hair. "You're okay sweetheart."

"Luke, do you know where you are?" A deep voice boomed as another unfamiliar face stood over me. He had thick white hair supported by a trimmed beard, his eyes were a dull grey colour and his face was full of wrinkles. I shook my head, I didn't know where I was or why I was here. "You're in the hospital." I glanced down at my body noticing all the wires and tubes connected from me to various machines that constantly beeped. There were several needles poking out of my hands and arms.

"You fell and hit your head when we went to that abandoned asylum!" Another familiar voice chirped in. I instantly followed the sound of the voice. The brown hair, hazel eyes and sweet smile were recognisable anywhere. "J-j-Jai?" My mouth hung open as my voice shook. He was stood right next to me, alive. No cuts, no bruises. He looked happy and healthy.

"Y-Y-ou're alive?" My bottom lip quivered as tears pricked at my dry eyes, the beeping from the machines indicating that my heart rate had began to speed up.

"Why wouldn't I be?" He chuckled, holding my hand gently in his.

Chapter 32

Luke's POV

Tears streamed my face like a waterfall, I glanced around the room observing my surroundings. Mum sat besides me running her hand soothingly through my curls, Beau stood behind her with a giant smile plastered on his face, Jai stood next to my beside with his hand firmly in mine and at the end of the bed stood an elderly looking doctor in a long white coat.

"Can you tell me what the date is?" The doctor questioned, he held a wooden clip board in his hand which I'm assuming contained my details.

I couldn't answer his question as I didn't know what the date was, I didn't even know what happened for me to end up in this place to begin with! I simply shook my head which he replied with a simple nod.

I glanced back up at Jai as I studied his features, he looked completely healthy and happy, he and Beau looked to be on good terms too. None of them looked angry or upset with me either. "A-are you okay?" I whispered, gently rubbing my thumb over the back of Jai's hand.

He looked at me as if I were crazy which honestly confused me greatly. "Am I okay? You're the one who took a hit to the head and you're asking if I'm okay?" He chuckled. It was my turn to look at him as if he were crazy. "B-b-but you were missing? And B-beau hurt you! Y-you were dead!" I suddenly cried, the heart monitor instantly picking up its pace.

"Calm down Luke." The doctor firmly ordered as he peered over his small glades up to the screen of the heat monitor.

How could they tell me to calm down! Didn't they know what happened!

"Luke, you suffered an extremely traumatic injury to your head. We had no option other than to medically induce you into a coma to help with the healing. The events you just described are all part of your imagination. You have been here for the past few months." The doctor explained.

I felt dizzy, everything that happened, Jai going missing, Beau hurting him, Jai dying, it was all part of my imagination. They didn't really happen, they weren't real. I felt a strong sense of relief wash over me. My Jai was fine, he was safe.

"I-i thought I lost you!" I cried, carefully pulling Jai towards me as I embraced him into a bone crushing hug. "Hey don't worry about me! I'm fine! You're the one who got hurt!" He mumbled into my shoulder as his arms wrapped around me. Beau soon joined into the hug, his smile never leaving his face.

"Do you really not remember what happened?" Beau questioned whilst raising his eyebrow.

Truth was I honestly had no idea what had happened, the only memories I had were that of my brain had created whilst I had been out of it.

"We went to film a video for the fans at the abandoned asylum, Jai pulled a prank on all of us and hid in the building and you freaked! You made us all search the place and whilst you and James went to search the top floor, the staircase collapsed with the both of you on it. James only had a few cuts and bruises but a piece of debris came down and knocked you out. We called the ambulance and you've been here since." Beau explained, taking a seat on the end of the bed but being careful of all the wires.

It took me a few moments to process his words. The events that took place in my imagination had seemed so realistic and had fooled me into thinking they were actually real when in reality they were all basically a big dream.

"S-so your okay?" I questioned, gently placing my hand against Jai's cheek. Jai nodded with his big grin as he placed his hand on top of mine. "I'm okay." He whispered in reply.